I. 1

Enter Orsino, Duke of Illyria, Curio, and other Lords.
DUKE: If music be the food of Love, play on,
　Give me excess of it: that surfeiting,
　The appetite may sicken, and so die.
　That strain again, it had a dying fall:
　O, it came o'er my ear, like the sweet sound
　That breathes upon a bank of violets;
　Stealing, and giving odour. Enough, no more,
　'Tis not so sweet now, as it was before.
　O spirit of Love, how quick and fresh art thou,
　That notwithstanding thy capacity,
　Receiveth as the sea, nought enters there,
　Of what validity, and pitch soe'er,
　But falls into abatement, and low price
　Even in a minute; so full of shapes is fancy,
　That it alone, is high fantastical.
CURIO: Will you go hunt my Lord?
DUKE: What Curio?
CURIO: The hart.
DUKE: Why so I do, the noblest that I have:
　O when mine eyes did see Olivia first,
　Methought she purg'd the air of pestilence;
　That instant was I turn'd into a hart,
　And my desires like fell and cruel hounds,
　E'er since pursue me. How now what news from her?
　　　　　　Enter Valentine.
VALENTINE: So please my Lord, I might not be admitted,
　But from her handmaid do return this answer:
　The Element itself, till seven years' hence.

Shall not behold her face at ample view:
But like a cloistress she will veiled walk,
And water once a day her chamber round
With eye-offending brine: all this to season
A brother's dead love, which she would keep fresh
And lasting, in her sad remembrance.

DUKE: O she that hath a heart of that fine frame
To pay this debt of love but to a brother,
How will she love, when the rich golden shaft
Hath kill'd the flock of all affections else
That live in her. When liver, brain, and heart,
These sovereign thrones, are all suppli'd, and fill'd
Her sweet perfections with one self king:
Away before me, to sweet beds of flowers,
Love-thoughts lie rich, when canopi'd with bowers.

Exeunt.

I. 2

Enter Viola, a Captain, and Sailors.

VIOLA: What country, friends, is this?
CAPTAIN: This is Illyria Lady.
VIOLA: And what should I do in Illyria?
My brother he is in Elysium,
Perchance he is not drown'd: what think you sailors?
CAPTAIN: It is perchance that you yourself were saved.
VIOLA: O my poor brother, and so perchance may he be.
CAPTAIN: True Madam, and to comfort you with chance,
Assure yourself, after our ship did split,
When you, and those poor number saved with you,
Hung on our driving boat: I saw your brother
Most provident in peril, bind himself,
(Courage and hope both teaching him the practice)

To a strong mast, that liv'd upon the sea:
Where like Orion on the dolphin's back,
I saw him hold acquaintance with the waves,
So long as I could see.

VIOLA: For saying so, there's gold:
Mine own escape unfoldeth to my hope,
Whereto thy speech serves for authority
The like of him. Know'st thou this country?

CAPTAIN: Ay Madam well, for I was bred and born
Not three hours' travel from this very place.

VIOLA: Who governs here?

CAPTAIN: A noble Duke in nature, as in name.

VIOLA: What is his name?

CAPTAIN: Orsino.

VIOLA: Orsino: I have heard my father name him.
He was a bachelor then.

CAPTAIN: And so is now, or was so very late:
For but a month ago I went from hence,
And then 'twas fresh in murmur (as you know
What great ones do, the less will prattle of)
That he did seek the love of fair Olivia.

VIOLA: What's she?

CAPTAIN: A virtuous maid, the daughter of a Count
That died some twelvemonth since, then leaving her
In the protection of his son, her brother,
Who shortly also died: for whose dear love
(They say) she hath abjur'd the company
And sight   of men.

VIOLA: O that I serv'd that Lady,
And might not be delivered to the world
Till I had made mine own occasion mellow
What my estate is.

CAPTAIN: That were hard to compass,

Because she will admit no kind of suit,
No, not the Duke's.

VIOLA: There is a fair behaviour in thee Captain,
And though that nature, with a beauteous wall
Doth oft close in pollution: yet of thee
I will believe thou hast a mind that suits
With this thy fair and outward character.
I prithee (and I'll pay thee bounteously)
Conceal me what I am, and be my aid,
For such disguise as haply shall become
The form of my intent. I'll serve this Duke,
Thou shalt present me as an eunuch to him,
It may be worth thy pains: for I can sing,
And speak to him in many sorts of music,
That will allow me very worth his service.
What else may hap, to time I will commit,
Only shape thou thy silence to my wit.

CAPTAIN: Be you his eunuch, and your mute I'll be,
When my tongue blabs, then let mine eyes not see.

VIOLA: I thank thee: lead me on.

Exeunt.

I. 3

Enter Sir Toby, and Maria.

SIR TOBY: What a plague means my niece to take the death
of her brother thus? I am sure care's an enemy to life.

MARIA: By my troth Sir Toby, you must come in earlier
a' nights: your cousin, my Lady, takes great exceptions
to your ill hours.

SIR TOBY: Why let her except, before excepted.

MARIA: Ay, but you must confine yourself within the
modest limits of order.

SIR TOBY: Confine? I'll confine myself no finer than I am: these clothes are good enough to drink in, and so be these boots too: and they be not, let them hang themselves in their own straps.

MARIA: That quaffing and drinking will undo you: I heard my Lady talk of it yesterday: and of a foolish knight that you brought in one night here, to be her wooer.

SIR TOBY: Who, Sir Andrew Ague-cheek?

MARIA: Ay he.

SIR TOBY: He's as tall a man as any's in Illyria.

MARIA: What's that to th' purpose?

SIR TOBY: Why he has three thousand ducats a year.

MARIA: Ay, but he'll have but a year in all those ducats: he's a very fool, and a prodigal.

SIR TOBY: Fie, that you'll say so: he plays o' th' viol-de-gamboys, and speaks three or four languages word for word without book, and hath all the good gifts of nature.

MARIA: He hath indeed, almost natural: for besides that he's a fool, he's a great quarreller: and but that he hath the gift of a coward, to allay the gust he hath in quarrelling, 'tis thought among the prudent, he would quickly have the gift of a grave.

SIR TOBY: By this hand they are scoundrels and substractors that say so of him. Who are they?

MARIA: They that add moreover, that he's drunk nightly in your company.

SIR TOBY: With drinking healths to my niece: I'll drink to her as long as there is a passage in my throat, and drink in Illyria: he's a coward and a coystrill that will not drink to my niece till his brains turn o' th' toe, like a parish-top. What wench? Castiliano vulgo: for here comes Sir Andrew Agueface.

Enter Sir Andrew.

SIR ANDREW: Sir Toby Belch. How now Sir Toby Belch?

SIR TOBY: Sweet Sir Andrew.

SIR ANDREW: Bless you fair shrew.

MARIA: And you too sir.

SIR TOBY: Accost Sir Andrew, accost.

SIR ANDREW: What's that?

SIR TOBY: My niece's chambermaid.

SIR ANDREW: Good Mistress Accost, I desire better acquaintance.

MARIA: My name is Mary sir.

SIR ANDREW: Good Mistress Mary Accost.

SIR TOBY: You mistake knight: accost, is front her, board her, woo her, assail her.

SIR ANDREW: By my troth I would not undertake her in this company. Is that the meaning of accost?

MARIA: Fare you well gentlemen.

SIR TOBY: And thou let part so Sir Andrew, would thou mightst never draw sword again.

SIR ANDREW: And you part so mistress, I would I might never draw sword again: fair lady, do you think you have fools in hand?

MARIA: Sir, I have not you by th' hand.

SIR ANDREW: Marry but you shall have, and here's my hand.

MARIA: Now sir, thought is free: I pray you bring your hand to th' buttery-bar, and let it drink.

SIR ANDREW: Wherefore, sweet-heart? What's your metaphor?

MARIA: It's dry sir.

SIR ANDREW: Why I think so; I am not such an ass, but I can keep my hand dry. But what's your jest?

MARIA: A dry jest sir.

SIR ANDREW: Are you full of them?

MARIA: Ay sir, I have them at my fingers' ends: marry now I let go your hand, I am barren.

Exit Maria.

SIR TOBY: O knight, thou lack'st a cup of Canary: when did I see thee so put down?

SIR ANDREW: Never in your life I think, unless you see Canary put me down: methinks sometimes I have no more wit than a Christian, or an ordinary man has: but I am a great eater of beef, and I believe that does harm to my wit.

SIR TOBY: No question.

SIR ANDREW: And I thought that, I'd forswear it. I'll ride home to-morrow Sir Toby.

SIR TOBY: *Pourquoi* my dear knight?

SIR ANDREW: What is *pourquoi?* Do, or not do? I would I had bestowed that time in the tongues, that I have in fencing, dancing and bear-baiting: O had I but followed the Arts.

SIR TOBY: Then hadst thou had an excellent head of hair.

SIR ANDREW: Why, would that have mended my hair?

SIR TOBY: Past question, for thou seest it will not curl my nature.

SIR ANDREW: But it becomes me well enough, does't not?

SIR TOBY: Excellent, it hangs like flax on a distaff; and I hope to see a housewife take thee between her legs, and spin it off.

SIR ANDREW: Faith I'll home to-morrow Sir Toby, your niece will not be seen, or if she be it's four to one, she'll none of me: the Count himself here hard by, woos her.

SIR TOBY: She'll none o' th' Count, she'll not match above her degree, neither in estate, years, nor wit: I have heard her swear 't. Tut there's life in 't man.

SIR ANDREW: I'll stay a month longer. I am a fellow o' th' strangest mind i' th' world; I delight in Masques and Revels sometimes altogether.

SIR TOBY: Art thou good at these kickchawses, knight?

SIR ANDREW: As any man in Illyria, whatsoever he be, under the degree of my betters, and yet I will not compare with an old man.

SIR TOBY: What is thy excellence in a galliard, knight?

SIR ANDREW: Faith, I can cut a caper.

SIR TOBY: And I can cut the mutton to 't.

SIR ANDREW: And I think I have the back-trick, simply as strong as any man in Illyria.

SIR TOBY: Wherefore are these things hid? Wherefore have these gifts a curtain before 'em? Are they like to take dust, like Mistress Mall's picture? Why dost thou not go to church in a galliard, and come home in a coranto? My very walk should be a jig: I would not so much as make water but in a sink-a-pace: what dost thou mean? Is it a world to hide virtues in? I did think by the excellent constitution of thy leg, it was form'd under the star of a galliard.

SIR ANDREW: Ay, 'tis strong, and it does indifferent well in a flame-colour'd stock. Shall we set about some Revels?

SIR TOBY: What shall we do else: were we not born under Taurus?

SIR ANDREW: Taurus? That's sides and heart.

SIR TOBY: No sir, it is legs and thighs: let me see thee caper. Ha, higher: ha, ha, excellent.

Exeunt.

I. 4

Enter Valentine, and Viola in man's attire.

VALENTINE: If the Duke continue these favours towards you Cesario, you are like to be much advanc'd, he hath known you but three days, and already you are no stranger.

VIOLA: You either fear his humour, or my negligence, that you call in question the continuance of his love. Is he inconstant sir, in his favours?

VALENTINE: No believe me.

Enter Duke, Curio, and Attendants.

VIOLA: I thank you: here comes the Count.

DUKE: Who saw Cesario hoa?

VIOLA: On your attendance my Lord here.

DUKE: Stand you a while aloof. Cesario,
Thou know'st no less, but all: I have unclasp'd
To thee the book even of my secret soul.
Therefore good youth, address thy gait unto her,
Be not deni'd access, stand at her doors,
And tell them, there thy fixed foot shall grow
Till thou have audience.

VIOLA: Sure my noble Lord,
If she be so abandon'd to her sorrow
As it is spoke, she never will admit me.

DUKE: Be clamorous, and leap all civil bounds,
Rather than make unprofited return.

VIOLA: Say I do speak with her (my Lord) what then?

DUKE: O then, unfold the passion of my love,
Surprise her with discourse of my dear faith;
It shall become thee well to act my woes:
She will attend it better in thy youth,
Than in a nuntio's of more grave aspect.

VIOLA: I think not so, my Lord.

DUKE: Dear lad, believe it;
  For they shall yet belie thy happy years,
  That say thou art a man: Diana's lip
  Is not more smooth, and rubious: thy small pipe
  Is as the maiden's organ, shrill, and sound,
  And all is semblative a woman's part.
  I know thy constellation is right apt
  For this affair: some four or five attend him,
  All if you will: for I myself am best
  When least in company: prosper well in this,
  And thou shalt live as freely as thy Lord,
  To call his fortunes thine.

VIOLA: I'll do my best
  To woo your Lady: yet a barful strife,
  Whoe'er I woo, myself would be his wife.

                      Exeunt.

I.5

Enter Maria, and Clown.

MARIA: Nay, either tell me where thou hast been, or I
will not open my lips so wide as a bristle may enter, in
way of thy excuse: my Lady will hang thee for thy
absence.

CLOWN: Let her hang me: he that is well hang'd in this
world, needs to fear no colours.

MARIA: Make that good.

CLOWN: He shall see none to fear.

MARIA: A good lenten answer: I can tell thee where that
saying was born, of I fear no colours.

CLOWN: Where good Mistress Mary?

MARIA: In the wars, and that may you be bold to say in your foolery.

CLOWN: Well, God give them wisdom that have it: and those that are fools, let them use their talents.

MARIA: Yet you will be hang'd for being so long absent, or be turn'd away: is not that as good as a hanging to you?

CLOWN: Many a good hanging, prevents a bad marriage: and for turning away, let summer bear it out.

MARIA: You are resolute then?

CLOWN: Not so neither, but I am resolv'd on two points.

MARIA: That if one break, the other will hold: or if both break, your gaskins fall.

CLOWN: Apt in good faith, very apt: well go thy way, if Sir Toby would leave drinking, thou wert as witty a piece of Eve's flesh, as any in Illyria.

MARIA: Peace you rogue, no more o' that: here comes my Lady: make your excuse wisely, you were best.

Exit.

Enter Lady Olivia, with Malvolio.

CLOWN: Wit, and't be thy will, put me into good fooling: those wits that think they have thee, do very oft prove fools: and I that am sure I lack thee, may pass for a wise man. For what says Quinapalus, Better a witty fool, than a foolish wit.   God bless thee Lady.

OLIVIA: Take the fool away.

CLOWN: Do you not hear fellows, take away the Lady.

OLIVIA: Go to, y'are a dry fool: I'll no more of you: besides you grow dishonest.

CLOWN: Two faults Madonna, that drink and good counsel will amend: for give the dry fool drink, then is the fool not dry: bid the dishonest man mend himself, if he mend, he is no longer dishonest; if he cannot, let the botcher mend him: anything that's mended, is but patch'd: virtue that transgresses, is but patch'd with sin, and sin that amends, is but patch'd with virtue. If that this simple syllogism will serve, so: if it will not, what remedy? As there is no true cuckold but calamity, so beauty's a flower; the Lady bade take away the fool, therefore I say again, take her away.

OLIVIA: Sir, I bade them take away you.

CLOWN: Misprision in the highest degree. Lady, *Cucullus non facit monachum*: that's as much to say, as I wear not motley in my brain: good Madonna, give me leave to prove you a fool.

OLIVIA: Can you do it?

CLOWN: Dexteriously, good Madonna.

OLIVIA: Make your proof.

CLOWN: I must catechize you for it Madonna. Good my Mouse of virtue answer me.

OLIVIA: Well sir, for want of other idleness, I'll bide your proof.

CLOWN: Good Madonna, why mourn'st thou?

OLIVIA: Good fool, for my brother's death.

CLOWN: I think his soul is in hell, Madonna.

OLIVIA: I know his soul is in heaven, fool.

CLOWN: The more fool, Madonna, to mourn for your brother's soul, being in heaven. Take away the fool, gentlemen.

OLIVIA: What think you of this fool Malvolio, doth he not mend?

MALVOLIO: Yes, and shall do, till the pangs of death shake him: infirmity that decays the wise, doth ever make the better fool.

CLOWN: God send you sir, a speedy infirmity, for the

better increasing your folly: Sir Toby will be sworn
that I am no fox, but he will not pass his word for two
pence that you are no fool.

OLIVIA: How say you to that Malvolio?

MALVOLIO: I marvel your Ladyship takes delight in such
a barren rascal: I saw him put down the other day, with
an ordinary fool, that has no more brain than a stone.
Look you now, he's out of his guard already: unless you
laugh and minister occasion to him, he is gagg'd. I protest
I take these wise men, that crow so at these set kind of
fools, no better than the fools' zanies.

OLIVIA: O you are sick of self-love Malvolio, and taste
with a distemper'd appetite. To be generous, guiltless,
and of free disposition, is to take those things for bird-
bolts, that you deem cannon-bullets: there is no slander
in an allow'd fool, though he do nothing but rail; nor no
railing, in a known discreet man, though he do nothing
but reprove.

CLOWN: Now Mercury indue thee with leasing, for thou
speakest well of fools.

Enter Maria.

MARIA: Madam, there is at the gate, a young gentleman,
much desires to speak with you.

OLIVIA: From the Count Orsino, is it?

MARIA: I know not, Madam, 'tis a fair young man, and
well attended.

OLIVIA: Who of my people hold him in delay?

MARIA: Sir Toby Madam, your kinsman.

OLIVIA: Fetch him off I pray you, he speaks nothing but
madman: fie on him. [*Exit Maria.*] Go you Malvolio; if
it be a suit from the Count, I am sick, or not at home.
What you will, to dismiss it. [*Exit Malvolio.*] Now you
see sir, how your fooling grows old, and people dislike it.

CLOWN: Thou hast spoke for us, Madonna, as if thy eldest son should be a fool: whose skull, Jove cram with brains, for here he comes.

Enter Sir Toby.

One of thy kin has a most weak *pia mater*.

OLIVIA: By mine honour half drunk. What is he at the gate cousin?

SIR TOBY: A gentleman.

OLIVIA: A gentleman? What gentleman?

SIR TOBY: 'Tis a gentleman here. A plague o' these pickle-herring: how now sot.

CLOWN: Good Sir Toby.

OLIVIA: Cousin, cousin, how have you come so early by this lethargy?

SIR TOBY: Lechery, I defy lechery: there's one at the gate.

OLIVIA: Ay marry, what is he?

SIR TOBY: Let him be the devil and he will, I care not: give me faith say I. Well, it's all one.

Exit.

OLIVIA: What's a drunken man like, fool?

CLOWN: Like a drown'd man, a fool, and a mad man: one draught above heat, makes him a fool, the second mads him, and the third drowns him.

OLIVIA: Go thou and seek the crowner, and let him sit o' my coz; for he's in the third degree of drink: he's drown'd: go look after him.

CLOWN: He is but mad yet Madonna, and the fool shall look to the madman.

Exit.

Enter Malvolio.

MALVOLIO: Madam, yond young fellow swears he will speak with you. I told him you were sick, he takes on him to understand so much, and therefore comes to speak

with you. I told him you were asleep, he seems to have a
foreknowledge of that too, and therefore comes to speak
with you. What is to be said to him Lady, he's fortified
against any denial?

OLIVIA: Tell him, he shall not speak with me.

MALVOLIO: Has been told so: and he says he'll stand at
your door like a Sheriff's post, and be the supporter to a
bench, but he'll speak with you.

OLIVIA: What kind o' man is he?

MALVOLIO: Why of mankind.

OLIVIA: What manner of man?

MALVOLIO: Of very ill manner: he'll speak with you, will
you, or no.

OLIVIA: Of what personage, and years is he?

MALVOLIO: Not yet old enough for a man, nor young
enough for a boy: as a squash is before 'tis a peascod, or
a codling when 'tis almost an apple: 'tis with him in
standing water, between boy and man. He is very well-
favour'd, and he speaks very shrewishly: one would
think his mother's milk were scarce out of him:

OLIVIA: Let him approach: call in my gentlewoman.

MALVOLIO: Gentlewoman, my Lady calls.

Exit.

Enter Maria.

OLIVIA: Give me my veil: come throw it o'er my face,   SIDE 1
We'll once more hear Orsino's embassy.   SIDE 2

Enter Viola.

VIOLA: The honourable Lady of the house, which is she?

OLIVIA: Speak to me, I shall answer for her: your will?

VIOLA: Most radiant, exquisite, and unmatchable beauty.
I pray you tell me if this be the Lady of the house, for I
never saw her. I would be loath to cast away my speech:
for besides that it is excellently well penn'd, I have taken

great pains to con it. Good beauties, let me sustain no scorn; I am very comptible, even to the least sinister usage.

OLIVIA: Whence came you sir?

VIOLA: I can say little more than I have studied, and that question's out of my part. Good gentle one, give me modest assurance, if you be the Lady of the house, that I may proceed in my speech.

OLIVIA: Are you a comedian?

VIOLA: No my profound heart: and yet (by the very fangs of malice, I swear) I am not that I play. Are you the Lady of the house?

OLIVIA: If I do not usurp myself, I am.

VIOLA: Most certain, if you are she, you do usurp yourself: for what is yours to bestow, is not yours to reserve. But this is from my commission: I will on with my speech in your praise, and then show you the heart of my message.

OLIVIA: Come to what is important in't: I forgive you the praise.

VIOLA: Alas, I took great pains to study it, and 'tis poetical.

OLIVIA: It is the more like to be feigned, I pray you keep it in. I heard you were saucy at my gates, and allow'd your approach rather to wonder at you, than to hear you. If you be not mad, be gone: if you have reason, be brief: 'tis not that time of moon with me, to make one in so skipping a dialogue.

MARIA: Will you hoist sail sir, here lies your way.

VIOLA: No good swabber, I am to hull here a little longer. Some mollification for your giant, sweet Lady:

OLIVIA: Tell me your mind.

VIOLA: I am a messenger.

OLIVIA: Sure you have some hideous matter to deliver, when the courtesy of it is so fearful. Speak your office.

VIOLA: It alone concerns your ear: I bring no overture of war, no taxation of homage; I hold the olive in my hand: my words are as full of peace, as matter.

OLIVIA: Yet you began rudely. What are you? What would you?

VIOLA: The rudeness that hath appear'd in me, have I learn'd from my entertainment. What I am, and what I would, are as secret as maiden-head: to your ears, divinity; to any other's, profanation.

OLIVIA: Give us this place alone, we will hear this divinity.

Exit Maria.

Now sir, what is your text?

VIOLA: Most sweet Lady.

OLIVIA: A comfortable doctrine and much may be said of it. Where lies your text?

VIOLA: In Orsino's bosom.

OLIVIA: In his bosom? In what chapter of his bosom?

VIOLA: To answer by the method, in the first of his heart.

OLIVIA: O, I have read it: it is heresy. Have you no more to say?

VIOLA: Good Madam, let me see your face.

OLIVIA: Have you any commission from your Lord, to negotiate with my face: you are now out of your text: but we will draw the curtain, and show you the picture. Look you sir, such a one I was this present: is't not well done?

VIOLA: Excellently done, if God did all.

OLIVIA: 'Tis in grain sir, 'twill endure wind and weather.

VIOLA: 'Tis beauty truly blent, whose red and white,
Nature's own sweet, and cunning hand laid on:
Lady, you are the cruell'st she alive,
If you will lead these graces to the grave,
And leave the world no copy.

OLIVIA: O sir, I will not be so hard-hearted: I will give out
divers schedules of my beauty. It shall be inventoried and
every particle and utensil labell'd to my will: as, Item
two lips indifferent red: Item two grey eyes, with lids to
them: Item, one neck, one chin, and so forth. Were you
sent hither to praise me?

VIOLA: I see you what you are, you are too proud:
But if you were the devil, you are fair:
My Lord and master loves you: O such love
Could be but recompens'd, though you were crown'd
The nonpareil of beauty.

OLIVIA: How does he love me?

VIOLA: With adorations, fertile tears,
With groans that thunder love, with sighs of fire.

OLIVIA: Your Lord does know my mind, I cannot love
him:
Yet I suppose him virtuous, know him noble,
Of great estate, of fresh and stainless youth;
In voices well divulg'd, free, learn'd, and valiant,
And in dimension, and the shape of nature,
A gracious person; but yet I cannot love him:
He might have took his answer long ago.

VIOLA: If I did love you in my master's flame,
With such a suffering, such a deadly life:
In your denial, I would find no sense,
I would not understand it.

OLIVIA: Why, what would you?

VIOLA: Make me a willow cabin at your gate,
And call upon my soul within the house,
Write loyal cantons of contemned love,
And sing them loud even in the dead of night:
Hallo your name to the reverberate hills,
And make the babbling gossip of the air,

Cry out Olivia: O you should not rest
Between the elements of air, and earth,
But you should pity me.

OLIVIA: You might do much:
What is your parentage?

VIOLA: Above my fortunes, yet my state is well:
I am a gentleman.

OLIVIA: Get you to your Lord:
I cannot love him: let him send no more,
Unless (perchance) you come to me again,
To tell me how he takes it: fare you well:
I thank you for your pains: spend this for me.

VIOLA: I am no fee'd post, Lady; keep your purse,
My master, not myself, lacks recompense.
Love make his heart of flint, that you shall love,
And let your fervour like my master's be,
Plac'd in contempt: farewell fair cruelty.

Exit.

OLIVIA: What is your parentage?
Above my fortunes, yet my state is well;
I am a gentleman. I'll be sworn thou art;
Thy tongue, thy face, thy limbs, actions, and spirit,
Do give thee five-fold blazon: not too fast: soft, soft,
Unless the master were the man. How now?
Even so quickly may one catch the plague?
Methinks I feel this youth's perfections
With an invisible, and subtle stealth
To creep in at mine eyes. Well, let it be.
What hoa, Malvolio.

Enter Malvolio.

MALVOLIO: Here Madam, at your service.

OLIVIA: Run after that same peevish messenger
The County's man: he left this ring behind him

Would I, or not: tell him, I'll none of it.
Desire him not to flatter with his Lord,
Nor hold him up with hopes, I am not for him:
If that the youth will come this way to-morrow,
I'll give him reasons for't: hie thee Malvolio.

MALVOLIO: Madam, I will.

Exit.

OLIVIA: I do I know not what, and fear to find
Mine eye too great a flatterer for my mind:
Fate, show thy force, ourselves we do not owe,
What is decreed, must be: and be this so.

Exit.

II. 1

Enter Antonio and Sebastian.

ANTONIO: Will you stay no longer: nor will you not that
I go with you?

SEBASTIAN: By your patience, no: my stars shine darkly
over me; the malignancy of my fate, might perhaps
distemper yours; therefore I shall crave of you your
leave, that I may bear my evils alone. It were a bad recompense for your love, to lay any of them on you.

ANTONIO: Let me yet know of you, whither you are
bound.

SEBASTIAN: No sooth sir: my determinate voyage is mere
extravagancy. But I perceive in you so excellent a touch
of modesty, that you will not extort from me, what I am
willing to keep in: therefore it charges me in manners,
the rather to express myself: you must know of me then
Antonio, my name is Sebastian (which I call'd Roderigo)
my father was that Sebastian of Messaline, whom I know
you have heard of. He left behind him, myself, and a

sister, both born in an hour: if the Heavens had been pleas'd, would we had so ended. But you sir, alter'd that, for some hour before you took me from the breach of the sea, was my sister drown'd.

ANTONIO: Alas the day.

SEBASTIAN: A Lady sir, though it was said she much resembled me, was yet of many accounted beautiful: but though I could not with such estimable wonder over-far believe that, yet thus far I will boldly publish her, she bore a mind that envy could not but call fair: she is drown'd already sir with salt water, though I seem to drown her remembrance again with more.

ANTONIO: Pardon me sir, your bad entertainment.

SEBASTIAN: O good Antonio, forgive me your trouble.

ANTONIO: If you will not murther me for my love, let me be your servant.

SEBASTIAN: If you will not undo what you have done, that is kill him, whom you have recover'd, desire it not. Fare ye well at once, my bosom is full of kindness, and I am yet so near the manners of my mother, that upon the least occasion more, mine eyes will tell tales of me: I am bound to the Count Orsino's Court, farewell.

Exit.

ANTONIO: The gentleness of all the gods go with thee:
I have many enemies in Orsino's Court,
Else would I very shortly see thee there:
But come what may, I do adore thee so,
That danger shall seem sport, and I will go.

Exit.

II. 2

Enter Viola and Malvolio, at several doors.

MALVOLIO: Were not you e'en now, with the Countess Olivia?

VIOLA: E'en now sir, on a moderate pace, I have since arriv'd but hither.

MALVOLIO: She returns this ring to you (sir) you might have saved me my pains, to have taken it away yourself. She adds moreover, that you should put your Lord into a desperate assurance, she will none of him. And one thing more, that you be never so hardy to come again in his affairs, unless it be to report your Lord's taking of this: receive it so.

VIOLA: She took the ring of me, I'll none of it.

MALVOLIO: Come sir, you peevishly threw it to her: and her will is, it should be so return'd: if it be worth stooping for, there it lies, in your eye: if not, be it his that finds it.

Exit.

VIOLA: I left no ring with her: what means this Lady?
Fortune forbid my outside have not charm'd her:
She made good view of me, indeed so much,
That as methought her eyes had lost her tongue,
For she did speak in starts distractedly.
She loves me sure, the cunning of her passion
Invites me in this churlish messenger:
None of my Lord's ring? Why he sent her none:
I am the man, if it be so, as 'tis,
Poor Lady, she were better love a dream:
Disguise, I see thou art a wickedness,
Wherein the pregnant enemy does much.

How easy is it, for the proper-false
In women's waxen hearts to set their forms:
Alas, our frailty is the cause, not we,
For such as we are made, of such we be:
How will this fadge? My master loves her dearly,
And I (poor monster) fond as much on him:
And she (mistaken) seems to dote on me:
What will become of this? As I am man,
My state is desperate for my master's love:
As I am woman (now alas the day)
What thriftless sighs shall poor Olivia breathe?
O time, thou must untangle this, not I,
It is too hard a knot for me t' untie.

Exit.

II. 3

Enter Sir Toby, and Sir Andrew.

SIR TOBY: Approach Sir Andrew: not to be a-bed after
midnight, is to be up betimes, and *diluculo surgere*, thou
know'st.

SIR ANDREW: Nay by my troth I know not: but I know,
to be up late, is to be up late.

SIR TOBY: A false conclusion: I hate it as an unfill'd can
To be up after midnight, and to go to bed then is early:
so that to go to bed after midnight, is to go to bed betimes. Does not our life consist of the four elements?

SIR ANDREW: Faith so they say, but I think it rather con-
sists of eating and drinking.

SIR TOBY: Th'art a scholar; let us therefore eat and drink.
Marian I say, a stoup of wine.

Enter Clown.

SIR ANDREW: Here comes the fool i' faith.

CLOWN: How now my hearts: did you never see the picture of we three?

SIR TOBY: Welcome ass, now let's have a catch.

SIR ANDREW: By my troth the fool has an excellent breast. I had rather than forty shillings I had such a leg, and so sweet a breath to sing, as the fool has. In sooth thou wast in very gracious fooling last night, when thou spok'st of Pigrogromitus, of the Vapians passing the Equinoctial of Queubus: 'twas very good i' faith: I sent thee sixpence for thy leman, hadst it?

CLOWN: I did impeticos thy gratillity: for Malvolio's nose is no whipstock: my lady has a white hand, and the Myrmidons are no bottle-ale houses.

SIR ANDREW: Excellent: why this is the best fooling, when all is done. Now a song.

SIR TOBY: Come on, there is sixpence for you. Let's have a song.

SIR ANDREW: There's a testril of me too: if one knight give a –

CLOWN: Would you have a love-song, or a song of good life?

SIR TOBY: A love-song, a love-song.

SIR ANDREW: Ay, ay. I care not for good life.

CLOWN [*sings*]:

O mistress mine where are you roaming?
O stay and hear, your true love's coming,
    That can sing both high and low.
Trip no further pretty sweeting;
Iourneys end in lovers meeting,
    Every wise man's son doth know.

SIR ANDREW: Excellent good, i' faith.

SIR TOBY: Good, good.

CLOWN [*sings*]:

What is love, 'tis not hereafter,
Present mirth, hath present laughter:
  What's to come, is still unsure.
In delay there lies no plenty,
Then come kiss me sweet and twenty:
  Youth's a stuff will not endure.

SIR ANDREW: A mellifluous voice, as I am true knight.

SIR TOBY: A contagious breath.

SIR ANDREW: Very sweet, and contagious i' faith.

SIR TOBY: To hear by the nose, it is dulcet in contagion. But shall we make the welkin dance indeed? Shall we rouse the night-owl in a catch, that will draw three souls out of one weaver? Shall we do that?

SIR ANDREW: And you love me, let's do't: I am a dog at a catch.

CLOWN: By'r lady sir, and some dogs will catch well.

SIR ANDREW: Most certain: let our catch be, *Thou knave.*

CLOWN: *Hold thy peace, thou knave* knight. I shall be constrain'd in't, to call thee knave, knight.

SIR ANDREW: 'Tis not the first time I have constrained one to call me knave. Begin fool: it begins, *Hold thy peace.*

CLOWN: I shall never begin if I hold my peace.

SIR ANDREW: Good i' faith: come begin.

Catch sung.
Enter Maria.

MARIA: What a caterwauling do you keep here? If my Lady have not call'd up her Steward Malvolio, and bid him turn you out of doors, never trust me.

SIR TOBY: My Lady's a Cataian, we are politicians, Malvolio's a Peg-a-Ramsey, and *Three merry men be we.* Am not I consanguineous? Am I not of her blood: tillyvally. Lady, *There dwelt a man in Babylon, Lady, Lady.*

CLOWN: Beshrew me, the knight's in admirable fooling.

SIR ANDREW: Ay, he does well enough if he be dispos'd, and so do I too: he does it with a better grace, but I do it more natural.

SIR TOBY: *O the twelfth day of December.*

MARIA: For the love o' God, peace.

Enter Malvolio.

MALVOLIO: My masters are you mad? Or what are you? Have you no wit, manners, nor honesty, but to gabble like tinkers at this time of night? Do ye make an alehouse of my Lady's house, that ye squeak out your coziers' catches without any mitigation or remorse of voice? Is there no respect of place, persons, nor time in you?

SIR TOBY: We did keep time sir in our catches. Sneck up.

MALVOLIO: Sir Toby, I must be round with you. My Lady bade me tell you, that though she harbours you as her kinsman, she's nothing alli'd to your disorders. If you can separate yourself and your misdemeanours, you are welcome to the house: if not, and it would please you to take leave of her, she is very willing to bid you farewell.

SIR TOBY: Farewell dear heart, since I must needs be gone.

MARIA: Nay good Sir Toby.

MALVOLIO: Is't even so?

SIR TOBY: But I will never die.

CLOWN: Sir Toby, there you lie.

MALVOLIO: This is much credit to you.

SIR TOBY: *Shall I bid him go?*

CLOWN: *What an if you do?*

SIR TOBY: *Shall I bid him go, and spare not?*

CLOWN: *O no, no, no, no, you dare not.*

SIR TOBY: Out o' tune sir, ye lie: art any more than a Steward? Dost thou think because thou art virtuous, there shall be no more cakes and ale?

CLOWN: Yes by Saint Anne, and ginger shall be hot i' th' mouth too.

SIR TOBY: Th'art i' th' right. Go sir, rub your chain with crums. A stoup of wine, Maria.

MALVOLIO: Mistress Mary, if you priz'd my Lady's favour at any thing more than contempt, you would not give means for this uncivil rule; she shall know of it by this hand.

Exit.

MARIA: Go shake your ears.

SIR ANDREW: 'Twere as good a deed as to drink when a man's a-hungry, to challenge him the field, and then to break promise with him, and make a fool of him.

SIR TOBY: Do't knight, I'll write thee a challenge: or I'll deliver thy indignation to him by word of mouth.

MARIA: Sweet Sir Toby be patient for to-night: since the youth of the Count's was to-day with my Lady, she is much out of quiet. For Monsieur Malvolio, let me alone with him: if I do not gull him into a nayword, and make him a common recreation, do not think I have wit enough to lie straight in my bed: I know I can do it.

SIR TOBY: Possess us, possess us, tell us something of him.

MARIA: Marry sir, sometimes he is a kind of Puritan.

SIR ANDREW: O, if I thought that, I'd beat him like a dog.

SIR TOBY: What for being a Puritan, thy exquisite reason, dear knight.

SIR ANDREW: I have no exquisite reason for't, but I have reason good enough.

MARIA: The devil a Puritan that he is, or any thing constantly but a time-pleaser, an affection'd ass, that cons state without book, and utters it by great swarths. The best persuaded of himself: so crammed (as he thinks) with excellencies, that it is his grounds of faith, that all that look on him, love him: and on that vice in him, will my revenge find notable cause to work.

SIR TOBY: What wilt thou do?

MARIA: I will drop in his way some obscure epistles of love, wherein by the colour of his beard, the shape of his leg, the manner of his gait, the expressure of his eye, forehead, and complexion, he shall find himself most feelingly personated. I can write very like my Lady your niece, on a forgotten matter we can hardly make distinction of our hands.

SIR TOBY: Excellent, I smell a device.

SIR ANDREW: I have't in my nose too.

SIR TOBY: He shall think by the letters that thou wilt drop that they come from my niece, and that she's in love with him.

MARIA: My purpose is indeed a horse of that colour.

SIR ANDREW: And your horse now would make him an ass.

MARIA: Ass, I doubt not.

SIR ANDREW: O 'twill be admirable.

MARIA: Sport royal I warrant you: I know my physic will work with him, I will plant you two, and let the fool make a third, where he shall find the letter: observe his construction of it: for this night to bed, and dream on the event: farewell.

Exit.

SIR TOBY: Good night Penthesilea.

SIR ANDREW: Before me she's a good wench.

SIR TOBY: She's a beagle true-bred, and one that adores me: what o' that?

SIR ANDREW: I was ador'd once too.

SIR TOBY: Let's to bed knight: thou hadst need send for more money.

SIR ANDREW: If I cannot recover your niece, I am a foul way out.

SIR TOBY: Send for money knight, if thou hast her not i' th' end, call me Cut.

SIR ANDREW: If I do not, never trust me, take it how you will.

SIR TOBY: Come, come, I'll go burn some sack, 'tis too late to go to bed now: come knight, come knight.

Exeunt.

II. 4

SIDE 2
SIDE 3

Enter Duke, Viola, Curio, and others.

DUKE: Give me some music: now good morrow friends.
Now good Cesario, but that piece of song,
That old and antique song we heard last night;
Methought it did relieve my passion much,
More than light airs, and recollected terms
Of these most brisk and giddy-paced times.
Come, but one verse.

CURIO: He is not here (so please your Lordship) that should sing it.

DUKE: Who was it?

CURIO: Feste the jester my Lord, a fool that the Lady Olivia's father took much delight in. He is about the house.

DUKE: Seek him out, and play the tune the while.

Exit Curio. Music plays.

Come hither boy, if ever thou shalt love
In the sweet pangs of it, remember me;
For such as I am, all true lovers are,

Unstaid and skittish in all motions else,
Save in the constant image of the creature
That is belov'd. How dost thou like this tune?
VIOLA: It gives a very echo to the seat
Where Love is thron'd.
DUKE: Thou dost speak masterly,
My life upon 't, young though thou art, thine eye
Hath stay'd upon some favour that it loves:
Hath it not boy?
VIOLA: A little, by your favour.
DUKE: What kind of woman is't?
VIOLA: Of your complexion.
DUKE: She is not worth thee then. What years i' faith?
VIOLA: About your years my Lord.
DUKE: Too old by heaven: let still the woman take
An elder than herself, so wears she to him;
So sways she level in her husband's heart:
For boy, however we do praise ourselves,
Our fancies are more giddy and unfirm,
More longing, wavering, sooner lost and won,
Than women's are.
VIOLA: I think it well my Lord.
DUKE: Then let thy love be younger than thyself,
Or thy affection cannot hold the bent:
For women are as roses, whose fair flower
Being once display'd, doth fall that very hour.
VIOLA: And so they are: alas, that they are so:
To die, even when they to perfection grow.·
                    Enter Curio and Clown.
DUKE: O fellow come, the song we had last night:
Mark it Cesario, it is old and plain;
The spinsters and the knitters in the sun,
And the free maids that weave their thread with bones,

Do use to chant it: it is silly sooth,
And dallies with the innocence of love,
Like the old age.

CLOWN: Are you ready sir?

DUKE: Ay prithee sing.

Music.
The Song.

CLOWN: *Come away, come away death,*
And in sad cypress let me be laid:
Fly away, fly away breath,
I am slain by a fair cruel maid:
My shroud of white, stuck all with yew,
O prepare it:
My part of death no one so true
Did share it.

Not a flower, not a flower sweet,
On my black coffin, let there be strown:
Not a friend, not a friend greet
My poor corpse, where my bones shall be thrown:
A thousand thousand sighs to save,
Lay me, O, where
Sad true lover never find my grave,
To weep there.

DUKE: There's for thy pains.

CLOWN: No pains sir, I take pleasure in singing sir.

DUKE: I'll pay thy pleasure then.

CLOWN: Truly sir, and pleasure will be paid one time, or another.

DUKE: Give me now leave, to leave thee.

CLOWN: Now the melancholy god protect thee, and the tailor make thy doublet of changeable taffeta, for thy mind is a very opal. I would have men of such constancy

put to sea, that their business might be every thing, and
their intent every where, for that's it, that always makes
a good voyage of nothing. Farewell.

Exit.

DUKE: Let all the rest give place: once more Cesario,
Get thee to yond same sovereign cruelty:
Tell her my love, more noble than the world
Prizes not quantity of dirty lands,
The parts that Fortune hath bestow'd upon her:
Tell her I hold as giddily as Fortune:
But 'tis that miracle and Queen of Gems
That nature pranks her in, attracts my soul.

VIOLA: But if she cannot love you sir?

DUKE: I cannot be so answer'd.

VIOLA: Sooth but you must.
Say that some Lady, as perhaps there is,
Hath for your love as great a pang of heart
As you have for Olivia: you cannot love her:
You tell her so: must she not then be answer'd?

DUKE: There is no woman's sides
Can bide the beating of so strong a passion,
As love doth give my heart: no woman's heart
So big, to hold so much, they lack retention.
Alas, their love may be call'd appetite,
No motion of the liver, but the palate,
That suffer surfeit, cloyment, and revolt,
But mine is all as hungry as the sea,
And can digest as much, make no compare
Between that love a woman can bear me,
And that I owe Olivia.

VIOLA: Ay but I know.

DUKE: What dost thou know?

VIOLA: Too well what love women to men **may** owe:

In faith they are as true of heart, as we.
My father had a daughter lov'd a man,
As it might be perhaps, were I a woman
I should your Lordship.

DUKE: And what's her history?

VIOLA: A blank my Lord: she never told her love,
But let concealment like a worm i' th' bud
Feed on her damask cheek: she pin'd in thought,
And with a green and yellow melancholy,
She sat like Patience on a Monument,
Smiling at grief. Was not this love indeed?
We men may say more, swear more, but indeed
Our shows are more than will: for still we prove
Much in our vows, but little in our love.

DUKE: But died thy sister of her love my boy?

VIOLA: I am all the daughters of my father's house,
And all the brothers too: and yet I know not.
Sir, shall I to this Lady?

DUKE: Ay that's the theme,
To her in haste: give her this jewel: say,
My love can give no place, bide no delay.

Exeunt.

II. 5

Enter Sir Toby, Sir Andrew, and Fabian.

SIR TOBY: Come thy ways Signior Fabian.

FABIAN: Nay I'll come: if I lose a scruple of this sport, let
me be boil'd to death with melancholy.

SIR TOBY: Wouldst thou not be glad to have the niggardly
rascally sheep-biter, come by some notable shame?

FABIAN: I would exult man: you know he brought me out
o' favour with my Lady, about a bear-baiting here.

SIR TOBY: To anger him we'll have the bear again, and we will fool him black and blue, shall we not Sir Andrew?

SIR ANDREW: And we do not, it is pity of our lives.

Enter Maria.

SIR TOBY: Here comes the little villain: how now my metal of India?

MARIA: Get ye all three into the box-tree: Malvolio's coming down this walk; he has been yonder i' the sun practising behaviour to his own shadow this half hour: observe him for the love of mockery: for I know this letter will make a contemplative idiot of him. Close in the name of jesting, lie thou there: for here comes the trout, that must be caught with tickling.

Exit.

Enter Malvolio.

MALVOLIO: 'Tis but Fortune, all is Fortune. Maria once told me she did affect me, and I have heard herself come thus near, that should she fancy, it should be one of my complexion. Besides she uses me with a more exalted respect, than any one else that follows her. What should I think on't?

SIR TOBY: Here's an overweening rogue.

FABIAN: Oh peace: contemplation makes a rare turkey-cock of him, how he jets under his advanc'd plumes.

SIR ANDREW: 'Slight I could so beat the rogue.

SIR TOBY: Peace I say.

MALVOLIO: To be Count Malvolio.

SIR TOBY: Oh rogue.

SIR ANDREW: Pistol him, pistol him.

SIR TOBY: Peace, peace.

MALVOLIO: There is example for't: the Lady of the Strachy, married the yeoman of the wardrobe.

SIR ANDREW: Fie on him Jezebel.

FABIAN: O peace, now he's deeply in: look how imagination blows him.

MALVOLIO: Having been three months married to her, sitting in my state.

SIR TOBY: O for a stone-bow to hit him in the eye.

MALVOLIO: Calling my officers about me, in my branch'd velvet gown: having come from a day-bed, where I have left Olivia sleeping.

SIR TOBY: Fire and brimstone.

FABIAN: O peace, peace.

MALVOLIO: And then to have the humour of state: and after a demure travel of regard: telling them I know my place, as I would they should do theirs: to ask for my kinsman Toby.

SIR TOBY: Bolts and shackles.

FABIAN: O peace, peace, peace, now, now.

MALVOLIO: Seven of my people with an obedient start, make out for him: I frown the while, and perchance wind up my watch, or play with my – some rich jewel: Toby approaches; courtesies there to me.

SIR TOBY: Shall this fellow live?

FABIAN: Though our silence be drawn from us with cars, yet peace.

MALVOLIO: I extend my hand to him thus: quenching my familiar smile with an austere regard of control.

SIR TOBY: And does not Toby take you a blow o' the lips, then?

MALVOLIO: Saying, Cousin Toby, my fortunes having cast me on your niece, give me this prerogative of speech.

SIR TOBY: What, what?

MALVOLIO: You must amend your drunkenness.

SIR TOBY: Out scab.

FABIAN: Nay patience, or we break the sinews of our plot.

MALVOLIO: Besides you waste the treasure of your time, with a foolish knight.

SIR ANDREW: That's me I warrant you.

MALVOLIO: One Sir Andrew.

SIR ANDREW: I knew 'twas I, for many do call me fool.

MALVOLIO: What employment have we here?

FABIAN: Now is the woodcock near the gin.

SIR TOBY: O peace, and the spirit of humours intimate reading aloud to him.

MALVOLIO: By my life this is my Lady's hand: these be her very *C's*, her *U's*, and her *T's*, and thus makes she her great *P's*. It is in contempt of question her hand.

SIR ANDREW: Her *C's*, her *U's*, and her *T's*: why that?

MALVOLIO: [*reads*] – *To the unknown beloved this and my good wishes*: her very phrases: by your leave wax. Soft, and the impressure her Lucrece, with which she uses to seal: 'tis my Lady: to whom should this be?

FABIAN: This wins him, liver and all.

MALVOLIO: *Jove knows I love, but who. Lips do not move, no man must know.* No man must know. What follows? the numbers alter'd: no man must know, if this should be thee Malvolio?

SIR TOBY: Marry hang thee brock.

MALVOLIO: *I may command where I adore,*
  But silence like a Lucrece knife:
With bloodless stroke my heart doth gore,
  M.O.A.I. doth sway my life.

FABIAN: A fustian riddle.

SIR TOBY: Excellent wench, say I.

MALVOLIO: *M. O. A. I.* doth sway my life. Nay but first let me see, let me see, let me see.

FABIAN: What dish a' poison has she dressed him?

SIR TOBY: And with what wing the staniel checks at it?

MALVOLIO: *I may command, where I adore:* Why she may command me: I serve her, she is my Lady. Why this is evident to any formal capacity. There is no obstruction in this, and the end: what should that alphabetical position portend, if I could make that resemble something in me? Softly, *M. O. A. I.*

SIR TOBY: O ay, make up that, he is now at a cold scent.

FABIAN: Sowter will cry upon't for all this, though it be as rank as a fox.

MALVOLIO: *M.* Malvolio, *M.* why that begins my name.

FABIAN: Did not I say he would work it out, the cur is excellent at faults.

MALVOLIO: *M.* But then there is no consonancy in the sequel, that suffers under probation: *A* should follow, but *O* does.

FABIAN: And *O* shall end, I hope.

SIR TOBY: Ay, or I'll cudgel him, and make him cry *O*.

MALVOLIO: And then *I* comes behind.

FABIAN: Ay, and you had any eye behind you, you might see more detraction at your heels, than fortunes before you.

MALVOLIO: *M, O, A, I.* This simulation is not as the former: and yet to crush this a little, it would bow to me, for every one of these letters are in my name. Soft, here follows prose:

If this fall into thy hand, revolve. In my stars I am above thee, but be not afraid of greatness: some are born great, some a-chieve greatness, and some have greatness thrust upon 'em. Thy fates open their hands, let thy blood and spirit embrace them, and to inure thyself to what thou art like to be: cast thy humble slough, and appear fresh. Be opposite with a kinsman, surly with servants: let thy tongue tang arguments of state; put thyself into the trick of singularity. She thus advises thee, that

sighs for thee. Remember who commended thy yellow stock-
ings, and wish'd to see thee ever cross-garter'd: I say remem-
ber, go to, thou art made if thou desirest to be so: if not, let me
see thee a steward still, the fellow of servants, and not worthy
to touch Fortune's fingers. Farewell. She that would alter
services with thee,

The Fortunate-Unhappy.

Daylight and champian discovers not more: this is open.
I will be proud, I will read politic authors, I will baffle
Sir Toby, I will wash off gross acquaintance, I will be
point-devise, the very man. I do not now fool myself, to
let imagination jade me; for every reason excites to this,
that my Lady loves me. She did commend my yellow
stockings of late, she did praise my leg being cross-garter'd, and in this she manifests herself to my love, and
with a kind of injunction drives me to these habits of her
liking. I thank my stars, I am happy: I will be strange,
stout, in yellow stockings, and cross-garter'd, even with
the swiftness of putting on. Jove, and my stars be praised.
Here is yet a postscript.

Thou canst not choose but know who I am. If thou entertain'st
my love, let it appear in thy smiling, thy smiles become thee
well. Therefore in my presence still smile, dear, my sweet, I
prithee.

Jove I thank thee, I will smile, I will do everything that
thou wilt have me.

Exit.

FABIAN: I will not give my part of this sport for a pension
of thousands to be paid from the Sophy.

SIR TOBY: I could marry this wench for this **device**.

SIR ANDREW: So could I too.

SIR TOBY: And ask no other dowry with her, but such another jest.

Enter Maria.

SIR ANDREW: Nor I neither.

FABIAN: Here comes my noble gull-catcher.

SIR TOBY: Wilt thou set thy foot o' my neck?

SIR ANDREW: Or o' mine either?

SIR TOBY: Shall I play my freedom at tray-trip, and become thy bond-slave?

SIR ANDREW: I' faith, or I either?

SIR TOBY: Why, thou hast put him in such a dream, that when the image of it leaves him, he must run mad.

MARIA: Nay but say true, does it work upon him?

SIR TOBY: Like aqua-vitæ with a midwife.

MARIA: If you will then see the fruits of the sport, mark his first approach before my Lady: he will come to her in yellow stockings, and it's a colour she abhors, and cross-garter'd, a fashion she detests: and he will smile upon her, which will now be so unsuitable to her disposition, being addicted to a melancholy, as she is, that it cannot but turn him into a notable contempt: if you will see it follow me.

SIR TOBY: To the gates of Tartar, thou most excellent devil of wit.

SIR ANDREW: I'll make one too.

Exeunt.

III. 1

SIDE 3
SIDE 4

Enter Viola and Clown.

VIOLA: Save thee friend and thy music: dost thou live by thy tabor?

CLOWN: No sir, I live by the Church.

VIOLA: Art thou a churchman?

CLOWN: No such matter sir, I do live by the Church: for,

I do live at my house, and my house doth stand by the Church.

VIOLA: So thou mayst say the King lies by a beggar, if a beggar dwell near him: or the Church stands by thy tabor, if thy tabor stand by the Church.

CLOWN: You have said sir: to see this age: a sentence is but a cheveril glove to a good wit, how quickly the wrong side may be turn'd outward.

VIOLA: Nay that's certain: they that dally nicely with words, may quickly make them wanton.

CLOWN: I would therefore my sister had had no name sir.

VIOLA: Why man?

CLOWN: Why sir, her name's a word, and to dally with that word might make my sister wanton: but indeed, words are very rascals, since bonds disgrac'd them.

VIOLA: Thy reason man?

CLOWN: Troth sir, I can yield you none without words, and words are grown so false, I am loath to prove reason with them.

VIOLA: I warrant thou art a merry fellow, and car'st for nothing.

CLOWN: Not so sir, I do care for something: but in my conscience sir, I do not care for you: if that be to care for nothing sir, I would it would make you invisible.

VIOLA: Art not thou the Lady Olivia's fool?

CLOWN: No indeed sir, the Lady Olivia has no folly, she will keep no fool sir, till she be married, and fools are as like husbands, as pilchers are to herrings, the husband's the bigger, I am indeed not her fool, but her corrupter of words.

VIOLA: I saw thee late at the Count Orsino's.

CLOWN: Foolery sir, does walk about the Orb like the Sun, it shines everywhere. I would be sorry sir, but the fool

should be as oft with your master, as with my mistress: I
think I saw your wisdom there.

VIOLA: Nay, and thou pass upon me, I'll no more with
thee. Hold there's expenses for thee.

CLOWN: Now Jove in his next commodity of hair, send
thee a beard.

VIOLA: By my troth I'll tell thee, I am almost sick for one,
though I would not have it grow on my chin. Is thy Lady
within?

CLOWN: Would not a pair of these have bred sir?

VIOLA: Yes being kept together, and put to use.

CLOWN: I would play Lord Pandarus of Phrygia sir, to
bring a Cressida to this Troilus.

VIOLA: I understand you sir, 'tis well begg'd.

CLOWN: The matter I hope is not great sir; begging, but a
beggar: Cressida was a beggar. My Lady is within sir. I
will conster to them whence you come, who you are,
and what you would are out of my welkin, I might say
element, but the word is overworn.

Exit.

VIOLA: This fellow is wise enough to play the fool,
And to do that well, craves a kind of wit:
He must observe their mood on whom he jests,
The quality of persons, and the time:
And like the haggard, check at every feather
That comes before his eye. This is a practice,
As full of labour as a wise man's art:
For folly that he wisely shows, is fit;
But wise men folly-fall'n, quite taint their **wit.**

Enter Sir Toby and Sir Andrew.

SIR TOBY. Save you gentleman.

VIOLA: And you sir.

SIR ANDREW: *Dieu vous garde Monsieur.*

VIOLA: *Et vous aussi votre serviteur.*

SIR ANDREW: I hope sir, you are, and I am yours.

SIR TOBY: Will you encounter the house, my niece is desir-
ous you should enter, if your trade be to her.

VIOLA: I am bound to your niece sir, I mean she is the list
of my voyage.

SIR TOBY: Taste your legs sir, put them to motion.

VIOLA: My legs do better understand me sir, than I understand what you mean by bidding me taste my legs.

SIR TOBY: I mean to go sir, to enter.

VIOLA: I will answer you with gait and entrance, but we
are prevented.

Enter Olivia and Gentlewoman.

Most excellent accomplish'd Lady, the heavens rain
odours on you.

SIR ANDREW: That youth's a rare Courtier, rain odours,
well.

VIOLA: My matter hath no voice Lady, but to your own
most pregnant and vouchsafed ear.

SIR ANDREW: Odours, pregnant, and vouchsafed: I'll get
'em all three all ready.

OLIVIA: Let the garden door be shut, and leave me to my
hearing. [*Exeunt Sir Toby, Sir Andrew, and Gentlewoman.*]
Give me your hand sir

VIOLA: My duty Madam, and most humble service.

OLIVIA: What is your name?

VIOLA: Cesario is your servant's name, fair Princess.

OLIVIA: My servant sir? 'Twas never merry world,
Since lowly feigning was call'd compliment:
Y'are servant to the Count Orsino youth.

VIOLA: And he is yours, and his must needs be yours:
Your servant's servant, is your servant Madam.

OLIVIA: For him, I think not on him: for his thoughts

Would they were blanks, rather than fill'd with me.
VIOLA: Madam, I come to whet your gentle thoughts
On his behalf.
OLIVIA: O by your leave I pray you.
I bade you never speak again of him;
But would you undertake another suit
I had rather hear you, to solicit that,
Than music from the spheres.
VIOLA: Dear Lady.
OLIVIA: Give me leave, beseech you: I did send,
After the last enchantment you did here,
A ring in chase of you. So did I abuse
Myself, my servant, and I fear me you:
Under your hard construction must I sit,
To force that on you in a shameful cunning
Which you knew none of yours. What might you think?
Have you not set mine honour at the stake,
And baited it with all th' unmuzzled thoughts
That tyrannous heart can think? To one of your receiving
Enough is shown, a cypress, not a bosom,
Hides my heart: so let me hear you speak.
VIOLA. I pity you.
OLIVIA: That's a degree to love.
VIOLA: No not a grize: for 'tis a vulgar proof
That very oft we pity enemies.
OLIVIA: Why then methinks 'tis time to smile again:
O world, how apt the poor are to be proud!
If one should be a prey, how much the better
To fall before the lion, than the wolf!
                    Clock strikes.
The clock upbraids me with the waste of time:
Be not afraid good youth, I will not have you,
And yet when wit and youth is come to harvest,

Your wife is like to reap a proper man:
There lies your way, due West.

VIOLA: Then westward-ho:
Grace and good disposition attend your Ladyship:
You'll nothing Madam to my Lord, by me?

OLIVIA: Stay: I prithee tell me what thou think'st of me?

VIOLA: That you do think you are not what you are.

OLIVIA: If I think so, I think the same of you.

VIOLA: Then think you right: I am not what I am.

OLIVIA: I would you were, as I would have you be.

VIOLA: Would it be better, Madam, than I am?
I wish it might, for now I am your fool.

OLIVIA: O what a deal of scorn, looks beautiful.
In the contempt and anger of his lip,
A murderous guilt shows not itself more soon,
Than love that would seem hid: Love's night, is noon.
Cesario, by the roses of the spring,
By maid-hood, honour, truth, and every thing,
I love thee so, that maugre all thy pride,
Nor wit, nor reason, can my passion hide:
Do not extort thy reasons from this clause,
For that I woo, thou therefore hast no cause:
But rather reason thus, with reason fetter;
Love sought, is good: but given unsought, is better.

VIOLA: By innocence I swear, and by my youth,
I have one heart, one bosom, and one truth,
And that no woman has, nor never none
Shall mistress be of it, save I alone.
And so adieu good Madam, never more,
Will I my master's tears to you deplore.

OLIVIA: Yet come again; for thou perhaps mayst move
That heart which now abhors, to like his love.

Exeunt.

III. 2

Enter Sir Toby, Sir Andrew, and Fabian.

SIR ANDREW: No faith, I'll not stay a jot longer.

SIR TOBY: Thy reason dear venom, give thy reason.

FABIAN: You must needs yield your reason, Sir Andrew.

SIR ANDREW: Marry I saw your niece do more favours to the Count's serving-man, than ever she bestow'd upon me: I saw't i' th' orchard.

SIR TOBY: Did she see thee the while, old boy, tell me that.

SIR ANDREW: As plain as I see you now.

FABIAN: This was a great argument of love in her toward you.

SIR ANDREW: S'light; will you make an ass o' me?

FABIAN: I will prove it legitimate sir, upon the oaths of judgement, and reason.

SIR TOBY: And they have been grand-jurymen, since before Noah was a sailor.

FABIAN: She did show favour to the youth in your sight, only to exasperate you, to awake your dormouse valour, to put fire in your heart, and brimstone in your liver: you should then have accosted her, and with some excellent jests, fire-new from the mint, you should have bang'd the youth into dumbness: this was look'd for at your hand, and this was balk'd: the double gilt of this opportunity you let time wash off, and you are now sail'd into the North of my Lady's opinion, where you will hang like an icicle on a Dutchman's beard, unless you do redeem it, by some laudable attempt, either of valour or policy.

SIR ANDREW: And't be any way, it must be with valour,

for policy I hate: I had as lief be a Brownist, as a politician.

SIR TOBY: Why then build me thy fortunes upon the basis of valour. Challenge me the Count's youth to fight with him, hurt him in eleven places, my niece shall take note of it, and assure thyself, there is no love-broker in the world, can more prevail in man's commendation with woman, than report of valour.

FABIAN: There is no way but this Sir Andrew.

SIR ANDREW: Will either of you bear me a challenge to him?

SIR TOBY: Go, write it in a martial hand, be curst and brief: it is no matter how witty, so it be eloquent, and full of invention: taunt him with the license of ink: if thou thou'st him some thrice, it shall not be amiss, and as many lies, as will lie in thy sheet of paper, although the sheet were big enough for the bed of Ware in England, set 'em down, go about it. Let there be gall enough in thy ink, though thou write with a goose-pen, no matter: about it.

SIR ANDREW: Where shall I find you?

SIR TOBY: We'll call thee at thy Cubicle: go.

Exit Sir Andrew.

FABIAN: This is a dear manakin to you Sir Toby.

SIR TOBY: I have been dear to him lad, some two thousand strong, or so.

FABIAN: We shall have a rare letter from him; but you'll not deliver't?

SIR TOBY: Never trust me then: and by all means stir on the youth to an answer. I think oxen and wainropes cannot hale them together. For Andrew, if he were open'd, and you find so much blood in his liver, as will clog the foot of a flea, I'll eat the rest of th' anatomy.

FABIAN: And his opposite the youth bears in his visage no
great presage of cruelty.

Enter Maria.

SIR TOBY: Look where the youngest wren of nine comes.

MARIA: If you desire the spleen, and will laugh yourselves
into stitches, follow me; yond gull Malvolio is turned
heathen, a very renegado; for there is no Christian that
means to be saved by believing rightly, can ever believe
such impossible passages of grossness. He's in yellow
stockings.

SIR TOBY: And cross-garter'd?

MARIA: Most villainously: like a pedant that keeps a school
i' th' Church: I have dogg'd him like his murtherer. He
does obey every point of the letter that I dropp'd, to be-
tray him: he does smile his face into more lines, than is in
the new map, with the augmentation of the Indies: you
have not seen such a thing as 'tis: I can hardly forbear
hurling things at him, I know my Lady will strike him:
if she do, he'll smile, and take't for a great favour.

SIR TOBY: Come bring us, bring us where he is.

Exeunt.

III. 3

Enter Sebastian and Antonio.

SEBASTIAN: I would not by my will have troubled you,
But since you make your pleasure of your pains,
I will no further chide you.

ANTONIO: I could not stay behind you: my desire
(More sharp than filed steel) did spur me forth,
And not all love to see you (though so much
As might have drawn one to a longer voyage)
But jealousy, what might befall your travel,

Being skilless in these parts: which to a stranger,
Unguided, and unfriended, often prove
Rough, and unhospitable. My willing love,
The rather by these arguments of fear
Set forth in your pursuit.
SEBASTIAN: My kind Antonio,
I can no other answer make, but thanks,
And thanks, and ever thanks; and oft good turns,
Are shuffl'd off with such uncurrent pay:
But were my worth, as is my conscience firm,
You should find better dealing: what's to do?
Shall we go see the reliques of this town?
ANTONIO: To-morrow sir, best first go see your lodging.
SEBASTIAN: I am not weary, and 'tis long to night:
I pray you let us satisfy our eyes
With the memorials, and the things of fame
That do renown this city.
ANTONIO: Would you'ld pardon me:
I do not without danger walk these streets.
Once in a sea-fight 'gainst the Count his galleys,
I did some service, of such note indeed,
That were I ta'en here, it would scarce be answer'd.
SEBASTIAN: Belike you slew great number of his people.
ANTONIO: Th' offence is not of such a bloody nature,
Albeit the quality of the time, and quarrel
Might well have given us bloody argument:
It might have since been answer'd in repaying
What we took from them, which for traffic's sake
Most of our city did. Only myself stood out,
For which if I be lapsed in this place
I shall pay dear.
SEBASTIAN: Do not then walk too open.
ANTONIO: It doth not fit me: hold sir, here's my purse.

In the south suburbs at the Elephant
Is best to lodge: I will bespeak our diet,
Whiles you beguile the time, and feed your knowledge
With viewing of the town, there shall you have me.
SEBASTIAN: Why I your purse?
ANTONIO: Haply your eye shall light upon some toy
   You have desire to purchase: and your store
   I think is not for idle markets, sir.
SEBASTIAN: I'll be your purse-bearer, and leave you
   For an hour.
ANTONIO: To th' Elephant.
SEBASTIAN: I do remember.
                        Exeunt.

III. 4

Enter Olivia and Maria.

OLIVIA: I have sent after him, he says he'll come:
   How shall I feast him? What bestow of him?
   For youth is bought more oft, than begg'd, or borrow'd.
   I speak too loud: Where's Malvolio, he is sad, and civil,
   And suits well for a servant with my fortunes,
   Where is Malvolio?
MARIA: He's coming Madam:
   But in very strange manner. He is sure possess'd Madam.
OLIVIA: Why what's the matter, does he rave?
MARIA: No Madam, he does nothing but smile: your
   Ladyship were best to have some guard about you, if he
   come, for sure the man is tainted in's wits.
OLIVIA: Go call him hither. [*Enter Malvolio.*]
   I am as mad as he,
   If sad and merry madness equal be.

How now Malvolio?

MALVOLIO: Sweet Lady, ho, ho.

OLIVIA: Smil'st thou? I sent for thee upon a sad occasion.

MALVOLIO: Sad Lady, I could be sad: this does make some
  obstruction in the blood: this cross-gartering, but what
  of that? If it please the eye of one, it is with me as the
  very true sonnet is: Please one, and please all.

MARIA: Why how dost thou man? what is the matter with
  thee?

MALVOLIO: Not black in my mind, though yellow in my
  legs: it did come to his hands, and commands shall be
  executed. I think we do know the sweet Roman hand.

OLIVIA: Wilt thou go to bed Malvolio?

MALVOLIO: To bed? Ay sweet-heart, and I'll come to
  thee.

OLIVIA: God comfort thee: why dost thou smile so, and
  kiss thy hand so oft?

MARIA: How do you Malvolio?

MALVOLIO: At your request: yes nightingales answer
  daws.

MARIA: Why appear you with this ridiculous boldness before my Lady?

MALVOLIO: Be not afraid of greatness: 'twas well writ.

OLIVIA: What mean'st thou by that Malvolio?

MALVOLIO: Some are born great.

OLIVIA: Ha?

MALVOLIO: Some achieve greatness.

OLIVIA: What say'st thou?

MALVOLIO: And some have greatness thrust upon them.

OLIVIA: Heaven restore thee.

MALVOLIO: Remember who commended thy yellow
  stockings.

OLIVIA: Thy yellow stockings?

MALVOLIO: And wish'd to see thee cross-garter'd.

OLIVIA: Cross-garter'd?

MALVOLIO: Go to, thou art made, if thou desirest to be so.

OLIVIA: Am I made?

MALVOLIO: If not, let me see thee a servant still.

OLIVIA: Why this is very midsummer madness.

Enter Servant.

SERVANT: Madam, the young gentleman of the Count Orsino's is return'd, I could hardly entreat him back: he attends your Ladyship's pleasure.

OLIVIA: I'll come to him. [*Exit Servant.*] Good Maria, let this fellow be look'd to. Where's my cousin Toby, let some of my people have a special care of him, I would not have him miscarry for the half of my dowry.

Exeunt Olivia and Maria.

MALVOLIO: O ho, do you come near me now: no worse man than Sir Toby to look to me. This concurs directly with the letter, she sends him on purpose, that I may appear stubborn to him: for she incites me to that in the letter. Cast thy humble slough says she: be opposite with a kinsman, surly with servants, let thy tongue tang with arguments of state, put thyself into the trick of singularity: and consequently sets down the manner how: as a sad face, a reverend carriage, a slow tongue, in the habit of some Sir of note, and so forth. I have lim'd her, but it is Jove's doing, and Jove make me thankful. And when she went away now, Let this fellow be look'd to: fellow? not Malvolio, nor after my degree, but fellow. Why every thing adheres together, that no dram of a scruple, no scruple of a scruple, no obstacle, no incredulous or unsafe circumstance: what can be said? Nothing that can be, can come between me, and the full prospect of my hopes. Well Jove, not I, is the doer of this, and he is to be thanked.

Enter Toby, Fabian and Maria.

SIR TOBY: Which way is he in the name of sanctity. If all the devils of hell be drawn in little, and Legion himself possess'd him, yet I'll speak to him.

FABIAN: Here he is, here he is: how is't with you sir? How is't with you man?

MALVOLIO: Go off, I discard you: let me enjoy my private: go off.

MARIA: Lo, how hollow the fiend speaks within him; did not I tell you? Sir Toby, my Lady prays you to have a care of him.

MALVOLIO: Ah ha, does she so?

SIR TOBY: Go to, go to: peace, peace, we must deal gently with him: let me alone. How do you Malvolio? How is't with you? What man, defy the devil: consider, he's an enemy to mankind.

MALVOLIO: Do you know what you say?

MARIA: La you, and you speak ill of the devil, how he takes it at heart. Pray God he be not bewitch'd.

FABIAN: Carry his water to th' wise woman.

MARIA: Marry and it shall be done to-morrow morning if I live. My Lady would not lose him for more than I'll say.

MALVOLIO: How now mistress?

MARIA: O Lord.

SIR TOBY: Prithee hold thy peace, this is not the way: do you not see you move him? Let me alone with him.

FABIAN: No way but gentleness, gently, gently: the Fiend is rough, and will not be roughly us'd.

SIR TOBY: Why how now my bawcock? how dost thou chuck?

MALVOLIO: Sir.

SIR TOBY: Ay Biddy, come with me. What man, 'tis not for gravity to play at cherry-pit with Satan. Hang him foul collier.

MARIA: Get him to say his prayers, good Sir Toby, get him to pray.

MALVOLIO: My prayers minx.

MARIA: No I warrant you, he will not hear of godliness.

MALVOLIO: Go hang yourselves all: you are idle shallow things, I am not of your element, you shall know more hereafter.

Exit.

SIR TOBY: Is't possible?

FABIAN: If this were played upon a stage now, I could condemn it as an improbable fiction.

SIR TOBY: His very genius hath taken the infection of the device man.

MARIA: Nay pursue him now, lest the device take air, and taint.

FABIAN: Why we shall make him mad indeed.

MARIA: The house will be the quieter.

SIR TOBY: Come, we'll have him in a dark room and bound. My niece is already in the belief that he's mad: we may carry it thus for our pleasure, and his penance, till our very pastime tir'd out of breath, prompt us to have mercy on him: at which time, we will bring the device to the bar and crown thee for a finder of madmen: but see, but see.

Enter Sir Andrew.

SIDE 4
SIDE 5

FABIAN: More matter for a May morning.

SIR ANDREW: Here's the challenge, read it: I warrant there's vinegar and pepper in't.

FABIAN: Is't so saucy?

SIR ANDREW: Ay, is't? I warrant him: do but read.

SIR TOBY: Give me. *Youth whatsoever thou art, thou art but a scurvy fellow.*

FABIAN: Good, and valiant.

SIR TOBY: *Wonder not, nor admire not in thy mind why I do call thee so, for I will show thee no reason for't.*

FABIAN: A good note, that keeps you from the blow of the Law.

SIR TOBY: *Thou com'st to the Lady Olivia, and in my sight she uses thee kindly: but thou liest in thy throat, that is not the matter I challenge thee for.*

FABIAN: Very brief, and to exceeding good sense – less.

SIR TOBY: *I will waylay thee going home, where if it be thy chance to kill me.*

FABIAN: Good.

SIR TOBY: *Thou kill'st me like a rogue and a villain.*

FABIAN: Still you keep o' th' windy side of the Law: good.

SIR TOBY: *Fare thee well, and God have mercy upon one of our souls. He may have mercy upon mine, but my hope is better, and so look to thyself. Thy friend as thou usest him, and thy sworn enemy,*

Andrew Aguecheek.

If this letter move him not, his legs cannot: I'll give't him.

MARIA: You may have very fit occasion for't: he is now in some commerce with my Lady, and will by and by depart.

SIR TOBY: Go Sir Andrew: scout me for him at the corner of the orchard like a bum-baily: so soon as ever thou seest him, draw, and as thou draw'st, swear horrible: for it comes to pass oft, that a terrible oath, with a swaggering accent sharply twang'd off, gives manhood more approbation, than ever proof itself would have earn'd him. Away.

SIR ANDREW: Nay let me alone for swearing.

Exit.

SIR TOBY: Now will not I deliver his letter: for the behaviour of the young gentleman, gives him out to be of good capacity, and breeding: his employment between his Lord and my niece, confirms no less. Therefore, this letter being so excellently ignorant, will breed no terror in the youth: he will find it comes from a clodpole. But sir, I will deliver his challenge by word of mouth; set upon Aguecheek a notable report of valour, and drive the gentleman (as I know his youth will aptly receive it) into a most hideous opinion of his rage, skill, fury, and impetuosity. This will so fright them both, that they will kill one another by the look, like cockatrices.

Enter Olivia and Viola.

FABIAN: Here he comes with your niece, give them way till he take leave, and presently after him.

SIR TOBY: I will meditate the while upon some horrid message for a challenge.

Exeunt Sir Toby, Fabian, and Maria.

OLIVIA: I have said too much unto a heart of stone,
And laid mine honour too unchary on't:
There's something in me that reproves my fault:
But such a headstrong potent fault it is,
That it but mocks reproof.

VIOLA: With the same haviour that your passion bears,
Goes on my master's grief.

OLIVIA: Here, wear this jewel for me, 'tis my picture:
Refuse it not, it hath no tongue, to vex you:
And I beseech you come again to-morrow.
What shall you ask of me that I'll deny,

That honour, sav'd, may upon asking give.

VIOLA: Nothing but this, your true love for my master.

OLIVIA: How with mine honour may I give him that,
Which I have given to you?

VIOLA: I will acquit you.

OLIVIA: Well, come again to-morrow: fare thee well,
A fiend like thee might bear my soul to hell.

Exit.

Enter Toby and Fabian.

SIR TOBY: Gentleman, God save thee.

VIOLA: And you sir.

SIR TOBY: That defence thou hast, betake thee to't: of
what nature the wrongs are thou hast done him, I know
not: but thy intercepter full of despite, bloody as the
hunter, attends thee at the orchard end: dismount thy
tuck, be yare in thy preparation, for thy assailant is quick,
skilful, and deadly.

VIOLA: You mistake sir I am sure, no man hath any quarrel
to me: my remembrance is very free and clear from any
image of offence done to any man.

SIR TOBY: You'll find it otherwise I assure you: therefore,
if you hold your life at any price, betake you to your
guard: for your opposite hath in him what youth,
strength, skill, and wrath, can furnish man withal.

VIOLA: I pray you sir what is he?

SIR TOBY: He is knight dubb'd with unhatch'd rapier, and
on carpet consideration, but he is a devil in private brawl,
souls and bodies hath he divorced three, and his incense-
ment at this moment is so implacable, that satisfaction can
be none, but by pangs of death and sepulchre: Hob, nob,
is his word: give't or take't.

VIOLA: I will return again into the house, and desire some
conduct of the Lady. I am no fighter, I have heard of

some kind of men, that put quarrels purposely on others, to taste their valour: belike this is a man of that quirk.

SIR TOBY: Sir, no: his indignation derives itself out of a very competent injury, therefore get you on, and give him his desire. Back you shall not to the house, unless you undertake that with me, which with as much safety you might answer him: therefore on, or strip your sword stark naked: for meddle you must that's certain, or forswear to wear iron about you.

VIOLA: This is as uncivil as strange. I beseech you do me this courteous office, as to know of the Knight what my offence to him is: it is something of my negligence, nothing of my purpose.

SIR TOBY: I will do so. Signior Fabian, stay you by this gentleman, till my return.

Exit,

VIOLA: Pray you sir, do you know of this matter?

FABIAN: I know the knight is incens'd against you, even to a mortal arbitrement, but nothing of the circumstance more.

VIOLA: I beseech you what manner of man is he?

FABIAN: Nothing of that wonderful promise to read him by his form, as you are like to find him in the proof of his valour. He is indeed sir, the most skilful, bloody, and fatal opposite that you could possibly have found in any part of Illyria: will you walk towards him, I will make your peace with him, if I can.

VIOLA: I shall be much bound to you for't: I am one, that had rather go with Sir Priest than Sir Knight: I care not who knows so much of my mettle.

Exeunt.
Enter Toby and Andrew.

SIR TOBY: Why man he's a very devil, I have not seen such

a firago: I had a pass with him, rapier, scabbard, and all:
and he gives me the stuck in with such a mortal motion
that it is inevitable: and on the answer, he pays you as
surely, as your feet hit the ground they step on. They
say, he has been fencer to the Sophy.

SIR ANDREW: Pox on't, I'll not meddle with him.

SIR TOBY: Ay but he will not now be pacified, Fabian can
scarce hold him yonder.

SIR ANDREW: Plague on't, and I thought he had been valiant, and so cunning in fence, I'd have seen him damn'd
ere I'd have challeng'd him. Let him let the matter slip,
and I'll give him my horse, grey Capilet.

SIR TOBY: I'll make the motion: stand here, make a good
show on't, this shall end without the perdition of souls.
Marry I'll ride your horse as well as I ride you.

Enter Fabian and Viola.

I have his horse to take up the quarrel, I have persuaded
him the youth's a devil.

FABIAN: He is as horribly conceited of him: and pants, and
looks pale, as if a bear were at his heels.

SIR TOBY: There's no remedy sir, he will fight with you
for's oath's sake: marry he hath better bethought him of
his quarrel, and he finds that now scarce to be worth talk-
ing of: therefore draw for the supportance of his vow, he
protests he will not hurt you.

VIOLA: Pray God defend me: a little thing would make
me tell them how much I lack of a man.

FABIAN: Give ground if you see him furious.

SIR TOBY: Come Sir Andrew, there's no remedy, the gentleman will for his honour's sake have one bout with
you: he cannot by the Duello avoid it: but he has prom-
ised me, as he is a gentleman and a soldier, he will not
hurt you. Come on, to't.

SIR ANDREW: Pray God he keep his oath.
                    Enter Antonio.
VIOLA: I do assure you 'tis against my will.
                    They draw.
ANTONIO: Put up your sword: if this young gentleman
    Have done offence, I take the fault on me:
    If you offend him, I for him defy you.
SIR TOBY: You sir? Why, what are you?
ANTONIO: One sir, that for his love dares yet do more
    Than you have heard him brag to you he will.
SIR TOBY: Nay, if you be an undertaker, I am for you.
                    They draw,
                    Enter Officers,
FABIAN: O good Sir Toby hold: here come the officers.
SIR TOBY: I'll be with you anon.
VIOLA: Pray sir, put your sword up if you please.
SIR ANDREW: Marry will I sir: and for that I promis'd you
    I'll be as good as my word. He will bear you easily, and
    reins well.
1 OFFICER: This is the man, do thy office.
2 OFFICER: Antonio, I arrest thee at the suit of Count Or-
    sino.
ANTONIO: You do mistake me sir.
1 OFFICER: No sir, no jot: I know your favour well:
    Though now you have no sea-cap on your head:
    Take him away, he knows I know him well.
ANTONIO: I must obey. This comes with seeking you:
    But there's no remedy, I shall answer it:
    What will you do: now my necessity
    Makes me to ask you for my purse. It grieves me
    Much more, for what I cannot do for you,
    Than what befalls myself: you stand amaz'd,
    But be of comfort.

2 OFFICER: Come sir away.

ANTONIO: I must entreat of you some of that money.

VIOLA: What money sir?
  For the fair kindness you have show'd me here,
  And part being prompted by your present trouble,
  Out of my lean and low ability
  I'll lend you something: my having is not much,
  I'll make division of my present with you:
  Hold, there's half my coffer.

ANTONIO: Will you deny me now,
  Is't possible that my deserts to you
  Can lack persuasion? Do not tempt my misery,
  Lest that it make me so unsound a man
  As to upbraid you with those kindnesses
  That I have done for you.

VIOLA: I know of none,
  Nor know I you by voice, or any feature:
  I hate ingratitude more in a man,
  Than lying, vainness, babbling drunkenness,
  Or any taint of vice, whose strong corruption
  Inhabits our frail blood.

ANTONIO: Oh heavens themselves.

2 OFFICER: Come sir, I pray you go.

ANTONIO: Let me speak a little. This youth that you see
      here,
  I snatch'd one half out of the jaws of death,
  Reliev'd him with such sanctity of love;
  And to his image, which methought did promise
  Most venerable worth, did I devotion.

1 OFFICER: What's that to us, the time goes by: away.

ANTONIO: But oh, how vile an idol proves this god:
  Thou hast Sebastian done good feature, shame.
  In Nature, there's no blemish but the mind:

None can be call'd deform'd, but the unkind.
Virtue is beauty, but the beauteous evil
Are empty trunks, o'erflourish'd by the devil.
I OFFICER: The man grows mad, away with him: come,
    come sir.
ANTONIO: Lead me on.
                    Exit with Officers.
VIOLA: Methinks his words do from such passion fly
    That he believes himself, so do not I:
    Prove true imagination, oh prove true,
    That I dear brother, be now ta'en for you.
SIR TOBY: Come hither Knight, come hither Fabian: we'll
    whisper o'er a couplet or two of most sage saws.
VIOLA: He nam'd Sebastian: I my brother know
    Yet living in my glass: even such, and so
    In favour was my brother, and he went
    Still in this fashion, colour, ornament,
    For him I imitate: O if it prove,
    Tempests are kind, and salt waves fresh in love.
                    Exit.
SIR TOBY: A very dishonest paltry boy, and more a cow-
    ard than a hare, his dishonesty appears, in leaving his
    friend here in necessity, and denying him: and for his
    cowardship ask Fabian.
FABIAN: A coward, a most devout coward, religious in it.
SIR ANDREW: 'Slid I'll after him again, and beat him.
SIR TOBY: Do, cuff him soundly, but never draw thy
    sword.
SIR ANDREW: And I do not.
                    Exit.
FABIAN: Come, let's see the event.
SIR TOBY: I dare lay any money, 'twill be nothing yet.
                    Exeunt.

IV. 1

Enter Sebastian and Clown.

CLOWN: Will you make me believe, that I am not sent for
you?

SEBASTIAN: Go to, go to, thou art a foolish fellow, let me
be clear of thee.

CLOWN: Well held out i' faith: no, I do not know you, nor
I am not sent to you by my Lady, to bid you come speak
with her: nor your name is not Master Cesario, nor this
is not my nose neither: nothing that is so, is so.

SEBASTIAN: I prithee vent thy folly somewhere else, thou
know'st not me.

CLOWN: Vent my folly: he has heard that word of some
great man, and now applies it to a fool. Vent my folly:
I am afraid this great lubber the World will prove a Cock-
ney: I prithee now ungird thy strangeness, and tell me
what I shall vent to my Lady? Shall I vent to her that
thou art coming?

SEBASTIAN: I prithee foolish Greek depart from me.
There's money for thee, if you tarry longer, I shall give
worse payment.

CLOWN: By my troth thou hast an open hand: these wise
men that give fools money, get themselves a good report,
after fourteen years' purchase.

Enter Andrew, Toby, and Fabian.

SIR ANDREW: Now sir, have I met you again: there's for
you.

SEBASTIAN: Why there's for thee, and there, and there.
Are all the people mad?

SIR TOBY: Hold sir, or I'll throw your dagger o'er the
house.

CLOWN: This will I tell my Lady straight, I would not be
in some of your coats for two pence.

Exit.

SIR TOBY: Come on sir, hold.

SIR ANDREW: Nay let him alone, I'll go another way to
work with him: I'll have an action of battery against
him, if there be any law in Illyria: though I struck him
first, yet it's no matter for that.

SEBASTIAN: Let go thy hand.

SIR TOBY: Come sir, I will not let you go. Come my
young soldier put up your iron: you are well flesh'd:
come on.

SEBASTIAN: I will be free from thee. What wouldst thou
now?
If thou dar'st tempt me further, draw thy sword.

SIR TOBY: What, what? Nay then I must have an ounce or
two of this malapert blood from you.

Enter Olivia.

OLIVIA: Hold Toby, on thy life I charge thee hold.

SIR TOBY: Madam.

OLIVIA: Will it be ever thus? Ungracious wretch,
Fit for the mountains, and the barbarous caves,
Where manners ne'er were preach'd: out of my sight.
Be not offended, dear Cesario:
Rudesby be gone.

Exeunt Sir Toby, Sir Andrew, and Fabian.

I prithee gentle friend,
Let thy fair wisdom, not thy passion sway
In this uncivil, and unjust extent
Against thy peace. Go with me to my house,
And hear thou there how many fruitless pranks
This ruffian hath botch'd up, that thou thereby
Mayst smile at this: thou shalt not choose but go:

Do not deny, beshrew his soul for me,
He started one poor heart of mine, in thee.

SEBASTIAN: What relish is in this? How runs the stream?
Or I am mad, or else this is a dream:
Let fancy still my sense in Lethe steep,
If it be thus to dream, still let me sleep.

OLIVIA: Nay come I prithee, would thou'ldst be rul'd by
me.

SEBASTIAN: Madam, I will.

OLIVIA: O say so, and so be.

Exeunt.

IV. 2

Enter Maria and Clown.

MARIA: Nay, I prithee put on this gown, and this beard,
make him believe thou art Sir Topas the Curate: do it
quickly. I'll call Sir Toby the whilst.

Exit.

CLOWN: Well, I'll put it on, and I will dissemble myself
in't, and I would I were the first that ever dissembled in
such a gown. I am not tall enough to become the function well, nor lean enough to be thought a good student:
but to be said an honest man and a good housekeeper
goes as fairly, as to say, a careful man, and a great scholar.
The competitors enter.

Enter Toby and Maria.

SIR TOBY: Jove bless thee Master Parson.

CLOWN: *Bonos dies* Sir Toby: for as the old hermit of
Prague that never saw pen and ink, very wittily said to
a niece of King Gorboduc, That that is, is: so I being
Master Parson, am Master Parson: for what is that, but
that? and is, but is?

SIR TOBY: To him Sir Topas.

CLOWN: What hoa, I say, Peace in this prison.

SIR TOBY: The knave counterfeits well: a good knave.
Malvolio within.

MALVOLIO: Who calls there?

CLOWN: Sir Topas the Curate, who comes to visit Malvolio the lunatic.

MALVOLIO: Sir Topas, Sir Topas, good Sir Topas go to
my Lady.

CLOWN: Out hyperbolical fiend, how vexest thou this
man? Talkest thou nothing but of Ladies?

SIR TOBY: Well said Master Parson.

MALVOLIO: Sir Topas, never was man thus wronged,
good Sir Topas do not think I am mad: they have laid
me here in hideous darkness.

CLOWN: Fie, thou dishonest Satan: I call thee by the most
modest terms, for I am one of those gentle ones, that will
use the devil himself with courtesy: sayest thou that
house is dark?

MALVOLIO: As hell Sir Topas.

CLOWN: Why, it hath bay windows transparent as barri-
cadoes, and the clearstores toward the south north, are as
lustrous as ebony: and yet complainest thou of obstruction?

MALVOLIO: I am not mad Sir Topas, I say to you this
house is dark.

CLOWN: Madman thou errest: I say there is no darkness
but ignorance, in which thou art more puzzl'd than the
Egyptians in their fog.

MALVOLIO: I say this house is as dark as ignorance, though
ignorance were as dark as hell; and I say there was never
man thus abus'd, I am no more mad than you are, make
the trial of it in any constant question.

CLOWN: What is the opinion of Pythagoras concerning wild fowl?

MALVOLIO: That the soul of our grandam, might happily inhabit a bird.

CLOWN: What thinkest thou of his opinion?

MALVOLIO: I think nobly of the soul, and no way approve his opinion.

CLOWN: Fare thee well: remain thou still in darkness, thou shalt hold th' opinion of Pythagoras, ere I will allow of thy wits, and fear to kill a woodcock, lest thou dispossess the soul of thy grandam. Fare thee well.

MALVOLIO: Sir Topas, Sir Topas.

SIR TOBY: My most exquisite Sir Topas.

CLOWN: Nay I am for all waters.

MARIA: Thou mightst have done this without thy beard and gown, he sees thee not.

SIR TOBY: To him in thine own voice, and bring me word how thou find'st him: I would we were well rid of this knavery. If he may be conveniently deliver'd, I would he were, for I am now so far in offence with my niece, that I cannot pursue with any safety this sport the upshot. Come by and by to my chamber.

Exeunt Sir Toby and Maria.

CLOWN: Hey Robin, jolly Robin,
Tell me how thy Lady does.

MALVOLIO: Fool.

CLOWN: My Lady is unkind, perdy.

MALVOLIO: Fool.

CLOWN: Alas why is she so?

MALVOLIO: Fool, I say.

CLOWN: She loves another. Who calls, ha?

MALVOLIO: Good fool, as ever thou wilt deserve well at my hand, help me to a candle, and pen, ink, and paper:

as I am a gentleman, I will live to be thankful to thee for't.

CLOWN: Master Malvolio?

MALVOLIO: Ay good fool.

CLOWN: Alas sir, how fell you besides your five wits?

MALVOLIO: Fool, there was never man so notoriously a-bus'd: I am as well in my wits, fool, as thou art.

CLOWN: But as well: then you are mad indeed, if you be no better in your wits than a fool.

MALVOLIO: They have here propertied me: keep me in darkness, send ministers to me, asses, and do all they can to face me out of my wits.

CLOWN: Advise you what you say: the minister is here. Malvolio, Malvolio, thy wits the heavens restore: endeavour thyself to sleep, and leave thy vain bibble babble.

MALVOLIO: Sir Topas.

CLOWN: Maintain no words with him good fellow. Who I sir, not I sir. God buy you good Sir Topas. Marry amen. I will, sir, I will.

MALVOLIO: Fool, fool, fool I say.

CLOWN: Alas sir be patient. What say you sir, I am shent for speaking to you.

MALVOLIO: Good fool, help me to some light, and some paper, I tell thee I am as well in my wits, as any man in Illyria.

CLOWN: Well-a-day, that you were sir.

MALVOLIO: By this hand I am: good fool, some ink, paper, and light: and convey what I will set down to my Lady: it shall advantage thee more, than ever the bearing of letter did.

CLOWN: I will help you to't. But tell me true, are you not mad indeed, or do you but counterfeit?

MALVOLIO: Believe me I am not, I tell thee true.

CLOWN: Nay, I'll ne'er believe a madman till I see his brains. I will fetch you light, and paper, and ink.

MALVOLIO: Fool, I'll requite it in the highest degree: I prithee be gone.

CLOWN: I am gone sir, and anon sir,
      I'll be with you again:
         In a trice, like to the old Vice,
      Your need to sustain.
      Who with dagger of lath, in his rage and his
         wrath,
         Cries ah ha, to the devil:
      Like a mad lad, pare thy nails dad,
         Adieu good man devil.

Exit.

IV. 3

Enter Sebastian.

SEBASTIAN: This is the air, that is the glorious Sun,
This pearl she gave me, I do feel't, and see't,
And though 'tis wonder that enwraps me thus,
Yet 'tis not madness. Where's Antonio then,
I could not find him at the Elephant,
Yet there he was, and there I found this credit,
That he did range the town to seek me out,
His counsel now might do me golden service,
For though my soul disputes well with my sense,
That this may be some error, but no madness,
Yet doth this accident and flood of Fortune,
So far exceed all instance, all discourse,
That I am ready to distrust mine eyes,
And wrangle with my reason that persuades me
To any other trust, but that I am mad,

Or else the Lady's mad; yet if 'twere so,
She could not sway her house, command her followers,
Take, and give back affairs, and their dispatch,
With such a smooth, discreet, and stable bearing
As I perceive she does: there's something in't
That is deceivable. But here the Lady comes.

Enter Olivia and Priest.

OLIVIA: Blame not this haste of mine: if you mean well
Now go with me, and with this holy man
Into the Chantry by: there before him,
And underneath that consecrated roof,
Plight me the full assurance of your faith,
That my most jealous, and too doubtful soul
May live at peace. He shall conceal it,
Whiles you are willing it shall come to note,
What time we will our celebration keep
According to my birth, what do you say?

SEBASTIAN: I'll follow this good man, and go with you,
And having sworn truth, ever will be true.

OLIVIA: Then lead the way good father, and heavens so
shine,
That they may fairly note this act of mine.

Exeunt.

V.I

SIDE 5
SIDE 6

Enter Clown and Fabian.

FABIAN: Now as thou lov'st me, let me see his letter.
CLOWN: Good Master Fabian, grant me another request.
FABIAN: Any thing.
CLOWN: Do not desire to see this letter.
FABIAN: This is to give a dog, and in recompense desire
my dog again.

Enter Duke, Viola, Curio, and Lords.

DUKE: Belong you to the Lady Olivia, friends?

CLOWN: Ay sir, we are some of her trappings.

DUKE: I know thee well: how doest thou my good fellow?

CLOWN: Truly sir, the better for my foes, and the worse for my friends.

DUKE: Just the contrary: the better for thy friends.

CLOWN: No sir, the worse.

DUKE: How can that be?

CLOWN: Marry sir, they praise me, and make an ass of me, now my foes tell me plainly, I am an ass: so that by my foes sir, I profit in the knowledge of myself, and by my friends I am abused: so that conclusions to be as kisses, if your four negatives make your two affirmatives, why then the worse for my friends, and the better for my foes.

DUKE: Why this is excellent.

CLOWN: By my troth sir, no: though it please you to be one of my friends.

DUKE: Thou shalt not be the worse for me, there's gold.

CLOWN: But that it would be double dealing sir, I would you could make it another.

DUKE: O you give me ill counsel.

CLOWN: Put your grace in your pocket sir, for this once, and let your flesh and blood obey it.

DUKE: Well, I will be so much a sinner to be a double dealer: there's another.

CLOWN: *Primo, secundo, tertio,* is a good play, and the old saying is, the third pays for all: the triplex sir, is a good tripping measure, or the bells of Saint Bennet sir, may put you in mind, one, two, three.

DUKE: You can fool no more money out of me at this throw: if you will let your Lady know I am here to speak

with her, and bring her along with you, it may awake
my bounty further.

CLOWN: Marry sir, lullaby to your bounty till I come a-
gain. I go sir, but I would not have you to think, that my
desire of having is the sin of covetousness: but as you say
sir, let your bounty take a nap, I will awake it anon.

Exit.

Enter Antonio and Officers.

VIOLA: Here comes the man sir, that did rescue me.

DUKE: That face of his I do remember well,
Yet when I saw it last, it was besmear'd
As black as Vulcan, in the smoke of war:
A bawbling vessel was he captain of,
For shallow draught and bulk unprizable,
With which such scathful grapple did he make,
With the most noble bottom of our fleet,
That very envy, and the tongue of loss
Cried fame and honour on him: what's the matter?

I OFFICER: Orsino, this is that Antonio
That took the *Phœnix*, and her fraught from Candy,
And this is he that did the *Tiger* board,
When your young nephew Titus lost his leg;
Here in the streets, desperate of shame and state,
In private brabble did we apprehend him.

VIOLA: He did me kindness sir, drew on my side,
But in conclusion put strange speech upon me,
I know not what 'twas, but distraction.

DUKE: Notable pirate, thou salt-water thief,
What foolish boldness brought thee to their mercies,
Whom thou in terms so bloody, and so dear
Hast made thine enemies?

ANTONIO: Orsino: noble sir,
Be pleas'd that I shake off these names you give me:

Antonio never yet was thief, or pirate,
Though I confess, on base and ground enough
Orsino's enemy. A witchcraft drew me hither:
That most ungrateful boy there by your side,
From the rude sea's enrag'd and foamy mouth
Did I redeem: a wrack past hope he was:
His life I gave him, and did thereto add
My love without retention, or restraint,
All his in dedication. For his sake,
Did I expose myself (pure for his love)
Into the danger of this adverse town,
Drew to defend him, when he was beset:
Where being apprehended, his false cunning
(Not meaning to partake with me in danger)
Taught him to face me out of his acquaintance,
And grew a twenty years removed thing
While one would wink: denied me mine own purse,
Which I had recommended to his use,
Not half an hour before.

VIOLA: How can this be?

DUKE: When came he to this town?

ANTONIO: To-day my Lord: and for three months before,
No interim, not a minute's vacancy,
Both day and night did we keep company.

Enter Olivia and Attendants.

DUKE: Here comes the Countess, now heaven walks on
earth:
But for thee fellow, fellow thy words are madness,
Three months this youth hath tended upon me,
But more of that anon. Take him aside.

OLIVIA: What would my Lord, but that he may not have,
Wherein Olivia may seem serviceable?
Cesario, you do not keep promise with me.

VIOLA: Madam.
DUKE: Gracious Olivia.
OLIVIA: What do you say Cesario? Good my Lord.
VIOLA: My Lord would speak, my duty hushes me.
OLIVIA: If it be aught to the old tune my Lord,
    It is as fat and fulsome to mine ear
    As howling after music.
DUKE: Still so cruel?
OLIVIA: Still so constant, Lord.
DUKE: What to perverseness? you uncivil Lady
    To whose ingrate, and unauspicious altars
    My soul the faithfull'st offerings hath breath'd out
    That e'er devotion tender'd. What shall I do?
OLIVIA: Even what it please my Lord, that shall become
        him.
DUKE: Why should I not, (had I the heart to do it)
    Like to th' Egyptian thief, at point of death
    Kill what I love: a savage jealousy,
    That sometime savours nobly: but hear me this:
    Since you to non-regardance cast my faith,
    And that I partly know the instrument
    That screws me from my true place in your favour:
    Live you the marble-breasted tyrant still.
    But this your minion, whom I know you love,
    And whom, by heaven I swear, I tender dearly,
    Him will I tear out of that cruel eye,
    Where he sits crowned in his master's spite.
    Come boy with me, my thoughts are ripe in mischief:
    I'll sacrifice the lamb that I do love,
    To spite a raven's heart within a dove.
VIOLA: And I most jocund, apt, and willingly,
    To do you rest, a thousand deaths would die.
OLIVIA: Where goes Cesario?

VIOLA: After him I love,
   More than I love these eyes, more than my life,
   More by all mores, than e'er I shall love wife.
   If I do feign, you witnesses above
   Punish my life, for tainting of my love.
OLIVIA: Ay me detested, how am I beguil'd?
VIOLA: Who does beguile you? who does do you wrong?
OLIVIA: Hast thou forgot thyself? Is it so long?
   Call forth the holy Father.
DUKE: Come, away.
OLIVIA: Whither my Lord? Cesario, husband, stay.
DUKE: Husband?
OLIVIA: Ay husband. Can he that deny?
DUKE: Her husband, sirrah?
VIOLA: No my Lord, not I.
OLIVIA: Alas, it is the baseness of thy fear,
   That makes thee strangle thy propriety:
   Fear not Cesario, take thy fortunes up,
   Be that thou know'st thou art, and then thou art
   As great as that thou fear'st.
                    Enter Priest.
   O welcome Father:
   Father, I charge thee by thy reverence
   Here to unfold, though lately we intended
   To keep in darkness, what occasion now
   Reveals before 'tis ripe: what thou dost know
   Hath newly pass'd, between this youth, and me.
PRIEST: A contract of eternal bond of love,
   Confirm'd by mutual joinder of your hands,
   Attested by the holy close of lips,
   Strengthen'd by interchangement of your rings,
   And all the ceremony of this compact
   Seal'd in my function, by my testimony:

Since when, my watch hath told me, toward my grave
I have travell'd but two hours.

DUKE: O thou dissembling cub: what wilt thou be
When time hath sow'd a grizzle on thy case?
Or will not else thy craft so quickly grow,
That thine own trip shall be thine overthrow:
Farewell, and take her, but direct thy feet,
Where thou, and I henceforth may never meet.

VIOLA: My Lord, I do protest.

OLIVIA: O do not swear,
Hold little faith, though thou hast too much fear.

Enter Sir Andrew.

SIR ANDREW: For the love of God a surgeon, send one
presently to Sir Toby.

OLIVIA: What's the matter?

SIR ANDREW: Has broke my head across, and has given
Sir Toby a bloody coxcomb too: for the love of God
your help, I had rather than forty pound I were at home.

OLIVIA: Who has done this Sir Andrew?

SIR ANDREW: The Count's gentleman, one Cesario: we
took him for a coward, but he's the very devil incardi-
nate.

DUKE: My gentleman Cesario?

SIR ANDREW: 'Od's lifelings here he is: you broke my
head for nothing, and that that I did, I was set on to do't
by Sir Toby.

VIOLA: Why do you speak to me? I never hurt you:
You drew your sword upon me without cause,
But I bespake you fair, and hurt you not.

Enter Sir Toby and Clown.

SIR ANDREW: If a bloody coxcomb be a hurt, you have
hurt me: I think you set nothing by a bloody coxcomb.
Here comes Sir Toby halting, you shall hear more: but if

he had not been in drink, he would have tickl'd you
othergates than he did.

DUKE: How now gentleman? how is't with you?

SIR TOBY: That's all one, has hurt me, and there's an end
on't: sot, didst see Dick Surgeon, sot?

CLOWN: O he's drunk Sir Toby an hour agone: his eyes
were set at eight i' th' morning.

SIR TOBY: Then he's a rogue, and a passy measures pavin:
I hate a drunken rogue.

OLIVIA: Away with him! Who hath made this havoc with
them?

SIR ANDREW: I'll help you Sir Toby, because we'll be
dress'd together.

SIR TOBY: Will you help an ass-head, and a coxcomb, and
a knave: a thin fac'd knave, a gull?

OLIVIA: Get him to bed, and let his hurt be look'd to.
  Exeunt Clown, Fabian, Sir Toby, and Sir Andrew.
    Enter Sebastian.

SEBASTIAN: I am sorry Madam I have hurt your kinsman:
But had it been the brother of my blood,
I must have done no less with wit and safety.
You throw a strange regard upon me, and by that
I do perceive it hath offended you:
Pardon me, sweet one, even for the vows
We made each other, but so late ago.

DUKE: One face, one voice, one habit, and two persons,
A natural perspective, that is, and is not.

SEBASTIAN: Antonio: O my dear Antonio,
How have the hours rack'd, and tortur'd me,
Since I have lost thee?

ANTONIO: Sebastian are you?

SEBASTIAN: Fear'st thou that Antonio?

ANTONIO: How have you made division of yourself?

An apple cleft in two, is not more twin
Than these two creatures. Which is Sebastian?
OLIVIA: Most wonderful.
SEBASTIAN: Do I stand there? I never had a brother:
    Nor can there be that deity in my nature
    Of here, and every where. I had a sister,
    Whom the blind waves and surges have devour'd:
    Of charity, what kin are you to me?
    What countryman? What name? What parentage?
VIOLA: Of Messaline: Sebastian was my father,
    Such a Sebastian was my brother too:
    So went he suited to his watery tomb:
    If spirits can assume both form and suit,
    You come to fright us.
SEBASTIAN: A spirit I am indeed,
    But am in that dimension grossly clad,
    Which from the womb I did participate.
    Were you a woman, as the rest goes even,
    I should my tears let fall upon your cheek,
    And say, Thrice-welcome drowned Viola.
VIOLA: My father had a mole upon his brow.
SEBASTIAN: And so had mine.
VIOLA: And died that day when Viola from her birth
    Had numbered thirteen years.
SEBASTIAN: O that record is lively in my soul,
    He finished indeed his mortal act
    That day that made my sister thirteen years.
VIOLA: If nothing lets to make us happy both,
    But this my masculine usurp'd attire:
    Do not embrace me, till each circumstance,
    Of place, time, fortune, do cohere and jump
    That I am Viola, which to confirm,
    I'll bring you to a captain in this town,

Where lie my maiden weeds: by whose gentle help,
I was preserv'd to serve this noble Count:
All the occurrence of my fortune since
Hath been between this Lady, and this Lord.

SEBASTIAN: So comes it Lady, you have been mistook:
But Nature to her bias drew in that.
You would have been contracted to a maid,
Nor are you therein (by my life) deceiv'd,
You are betroth'd both to a maid and man.

DUKE: Be not amaz'd, right noble is his blood:
If this be so, as yet the glass seems true,
I shall have share in this most happy wrack:
Boy, thou hast said to me a thousand times,
Thou never shouldst love woman like to me.

VIOLA: And all those sayings, will I over-swear,
And all those swearings keep as true in soul,
As doth that orbed continent, the fire,
That severs day from night.

DUKE: Give me thy hand,
And let me see thee in thy woman's weeds.

VIOLA: The captain that did bring me first on shore
Hath my maid's garments: he upon some action
Is now in durance, at Malvolio's suit,
A gentleman, and follower of my Lady's.

OLIVIA: He shall enlarge him: fetch Malvolio hither,
And yet alas, now I remember me,
They say poor gentleman, he's much distract.
            Enter Clown with a letter, and Fabian.
A most extracting frenzy of mine own
From my remembrance, clearly banish'd his.
How does he sirrah?

CLOWN: Truly Madam, he holds Belzebub at the stave's
end as well as a man in his case may do: has here writ a

letter to you, I should have given't you to-day morning.
But as a madman's Epistles are no Gospels, so it skills not
much when they are deliver'd.

OLIVIA: Open't, and read it.

CLOWN: Look then to be well edified, when the fool de-
livers the madman. *By the Lord Madam.*

OLIVIA: How now, art thou mad?

CLOWN: No Madam, I do but read madness: and your
Ladyship will have it as it ought to be, you must allow *Vox.*

OLIVIA: Prithee read i' thy right wits.

CLOWN: So I do Madonna: but to read his right wits, is to
read thus: therefore, perpend my Princess, and give ear.

OLIVIA: Read it you, sirrah.

FABIAN [*reads*]: *By the Lord Madam, you wrong me, and the
world shall know it: though you have put me into darkness,
and given your drunken cousin rule over me, yet have I the
benefit of my senses as well as your Ladyship. I have your own
letter, that induced me to the semblance I put on; with the
which I doubt not, but to do myself much right, or you much
shame: think of me as you please. I leave my duty a little un-
thought of, and speak out of my injury.*

The madly-us'd Malvolio.

OLIVIA: Did he write this?

CLOWN: Ay Madam.

DUKE: This savours not much of distraction.

OLIVIA: See him deliver'd Fabian, bring him hither:

Exit Fabian.

My Lord, so please you, these things further thought on,
To think me as well a sister, as a wife,
One day shall crown th' alliance on't, so please you,
Here at my house, and at my proper cost.

DUKE: Madam, I am most apt t' embrace your offer:
Your master quits you: and for your service done him,

So much against the mettle of your sex,
So far beneath your soft and tender breeding,
And since you call'd me master for so long:
Here is my hand, you shall from this time be
Your master's mistress.

OLIVIA: A sister, you are she.

> *Enter Malvolio and Fabian.*

DUKE: Is this the madman?

OLIVIA: Ay my Lord, this same: how now Malvolio?

MALVOLIO: Madam, you have done me wrong,
Notorious wrong.

OLIVIA: Have I Malvolio? No.

MALVOLIO: Lady you have, pray you peruse that letter.
You must not now deny it is your hand,
Write from it if you can, in hand, or phrase,
Or say, 'tis not your seal, not your invention:
You can say none of this. Well, grant it then,
And tell me in the modesty of honour,
Why you have given me such clear lights of favour,
Bade me come smiling, and cross-garter'd to you,
To put on yellow stockings, and to frown
Upon Sir Toby, and the lighter people:
And acting this in an obedient hope,
Why have you suffer'd me to be imprison'd,
Kept in a dark house, visited by the Priest,
And made the most notorious geck and gull,
That e'er invention play'd on? Tell me why?

OLIVIA: Alas Malvolio, this is not my writing,
Though I confess much like the character:
But out of question, 'tis Maria's hand.
And now I do bethink me, it was she
First told me thou wast mad; then cam'st in smiling,
And in such forms, which here were presuppos'd

Upon thee in the letter: prithee be content,
This practice hath most shrewdly pass'd upon thee:
But when we know the grounds, and authors of it,
Thou shalt be both the plaintiff and the judge
Of thine own cause.

FABIAN: Good Madam hear me speak,
And let no quarrel, nor no brawl to come,
Taint the condition of this present hour,
Which I have wonder'd at. In hope it shall not,
Most freely I confess myself, and Toby
Set this device against Malvolio here,
Upon some stubborn and uncourteous parts
We had conceiv'd against him. Maria writ
The letter, at Sir Toby's great importance,
In recompense whereof, he hath married her:
How with a sportful malice it was follow'd,
May rather pluck on laughter than revenge,
If that the injuries be justly weigh'd,
That have on both sides pass'd.

OLIVIA: Alas poor fool, how have they baffled thee?

CLOWN: Why some are born great, some achieve greatness, and some have greatness thrown upon them. I was
one sir, in this interlude, one Sir Topas sir, but that's all
one: by the Lord fool, I am not mad: but do you remember, Madam, why laugh you at such a barren rascal, and
you smile not he's gagg'd: and thus the whirligig of time
brings in his revenges.

MALVOLIO: I'll be reveng'd on the whole pack of you!
Exit.

OLIVIA: He hath been most notoriously abus'd.

DUKE: Pursue him, and entreat him to a peace:
He hath not told us of the captain yet,
When that is known, and golden time convents,

A solemn combination shall be made
Of our dear souls. Meantime sweet sister,
We will not part from hence. Cesario come
(For so you shall be while you are a man)
But when in other habits you are seen,
Orsino's Mistress, and his fancy's Queen.
                    Exeunt all but Clown.
CLOWN [*sings*]:
> *When that I was and a little tiny boy,*
>   *With hey ho, the wind and the rain:*
> *A foolish thing was but a toy,*
>   *For the rain it raineth every day.*
>
> *But when I came to man's estate.*
>   *With hey ho, &c.*
> *'Gainst knaves and thieves men shut their gate,*
>   *For the rain, &c.*
>
> *But when I came alas to wive,*
>   *With hey ho, &c.*
> *By swaggering could I never thrive,*
>   *For the rain, &c.*
>
> *But when I came unto my beds,*
>   *With hey ho, &c.*
> *With toss-pots still had drunken heads,*
>   *For the rain, &c.*
>
> *A great while ago the world begun,*
>   *With hey ho, &c.*
> *But that's all one, our Play is done,*
>   *And we'll strive to please you every day.*
>   *With hey ho, &c*
> *For the rain, &c.*

                    Exit.